No Mistletoe Kiss for a Cowboy

Book 6 in the Escape to Cowboy Crossing series

By Alexa Verde

---

1. https://sweetlibertydesigns.com/

About the book

A woman fighting to survive. A cowboy fighting for her. But news about her missing child could tear them apart...

.

After being brutally beaten up by her ex-husband and left helpless and jobless, Courtney Rogers reluctantly agrees to recover at the only safe haven she knows. A ranch where one of the cowboy brothers could steal her heart, if only it wasn't shattered.
Sean O'Neill crushed on Courtney since the moment the mysterious woman disappeared without trace. Now that she's back in his life—sort of—he's eager to help her heal.

.

When she decides to go to her ex to find the daughter he'd persuaded her was dead, can Sean and Courtney—and their love—survive?

~

Escape to Cowboy Crossing
Women scarred by their painful pasts, bonded like sisters by the secrets they share. Cowboys able to see the hurting hearts behind the tough facades. And someone willing to kill to get what they want...

Dedication

This book is dedicated to Mary Jane M., my wonderful reader who's been super supportive to me throughout the years. She's also always one of the first people to post reviews for my new books.
Thank you so much for your kindness, Mary Jane.

Chapter One

Goosebumps erupted on Courtney's skin.

This couldn't be happening. After all this time... She'd been so careful.

Except for today.

Lost in her thoughts about being alone at Christmas, she'd opened the door and disabled the security. He slipped inside before she locked the door, making her flinch and shudder.

How had she failed to hear the footsteps behind her? The crunching of snow? How?

She should scream, but her voice betrayed her. Besides, it would be no use. Somehow, she managed to slide her gloved hand into her purse. Close to the cold metal of the gun.

The man she'd once loved so much tsked as he turned on the light. "I wouldn't do that if I were you. Put your purse on the floor."

Right. Then she'd be defenseless. Like she'd been many times before.

"No!" Her voice came out raspy, unfamiliar. She wanted to pull out the weapon, but he was faster. Pain erupted in her cheekbone and her shoulder as he hit her and jerked the purse out of her hands.

"Is this the way to greet your husband?" His lips she'd kissed so many times before tugged up.

Once upon a time, she'd found that smile charming. Before she knew his true nature. He'd grown a beard and a mustache now, his raven-black hair reaching the collar of his new leather coat. But the leather boots... Those she knew well, from up close, and just how hard they could hit.

"Ex-husband," she grunted even as her cheek begged for some ice to reduce the pain. She tasted the saltiness of blood. He'd broken skin. This was just the beginning.

"I see you're all ready for Christmas." He plugged in the Christmas tree, and it lit up with red, green, and gold twinkles, mocking the horror of her situation. "But how can you spend Christmas without me, your *husband*? That wouldn't be right."

Could she make it to the bathroom fast enough to lock herself in? He'd just knock down the door. She'd seen him do so before. He pumped iron and took pride in his muscles and his fists. She knew just how heavy those fists were, too.

She shuddered but refused to cower. Not any longer. Not that it had ever helped anyway. "Ex-husband," she said again.

"Ex-husband. Don't remind me about your betrayal," he growled. Then he smiled derisively. "No presents under the tree, huh? Not even for me? You should've known I'd come for you."

Those Christmas lights winked at her again.

Would her neighbors hear her if she screamed? Sadly, the family on the left had gone to visit relatives for the holidays. The only neighbor on the right was a nurse and worked night shifts. What other options did she have?

"But *I* have a present for you. One you'd never expect." He shifted closer. The familiar scent of whiskey made her swallow hard as all hope seeped from her pores.

She couldn't reason with him when he was sober. When he was drunk... *Forget it.* A shiver traveled down her spine despite the warm coat. "I don't need your presents. Just leave. Please."

"You'd care for this one. It's something very dear to you." Menace appeared in his eyes.

What was he talking about? One of the many mementos she left behind when she'd fled? "You can keep it."

His eyes narrowed as he circled closer. "You wouldn't say that if you knew what it was. You wouldn't say that at all."

Her mind scrambled for a solution. Once, he'd persuaded her she was worthless, had made her give up her job and friends.

But she'd changed in the years without him. She'd returned to her job as a pilot, though she'd had to take on private charters, sometimes into dangerous territories, where few questions were asked, to keep as low a profile as possible. She'd even met a few people who seemed to care about her. Sean's face flashed in front of her, making her heart skip a beat. Sean's family was nice to her. Even if she'd had to push them away.

Maybe another of her mistakes, but then she'd made a lot of them. Besides, even if Sean had seemed caring, she couldn't trust her heart. Just look where it had led her.

"How dare you leave me?"

Her ex blocked the exit, so she couldn't run outside.

Her phone was in her purse, so she couldn't reach it.

She'd never make it to the kitchen in time to snatch a knife. And if she did, he'd just take it from her. She'd barely survived the beatings. She wouldn't survive a stabbing.

What was left?

Think.

The house she'd rented in a futile hope of starting over had an open floor plan, the entrance flowing into the living room. What was in the living room that she could use?

A sofa, bookshelves, a table...

Hold on. A table. She breathed in the faint scent of roses, a welcome distraction from the stink of whiskey. She had a bouquet on the table. A breath of life in the middle of winter, a reminder she could feel alive again one day and maybe even bloom.

How naïve those hopes seemed now.

She stepped back on the carpet, then another time. "You know why I left. Should I remind you about my broken ribs? Or my broken nose? Or all the bruises?"

"That was your fault!" He picked up a sparkling green tree ornament and threw it against the wall. Its shards shattered onto the floor like her heart once had.

"Why don't you go on with your life? Let me be?" Asking was useless, and she knew it. But she needed to buy some time.

His eyes narrowed, and no trace of a smile accentuated the face she'd once considered so handsome. "Because nobody leaves me!"

Another step back, muffled by the carpet. "I already did."

Aggravating him wasn't a good idea, but placating him wasn't possible, either. As she'd found out the hard way.

"You belong to me!" He advanced. Six feet tall, he towered over her, and it used to be so intimidating.

But she wasn't going to surrender without a fight now. "Not anymore." She whirled around, snatched the vase, and emptied it in his face.

As the water ran down his blazer, he gaped at her.

Gathering her strength, she hit him on the side of his head with the leaded crystal vase. Then she made a run for it.

Sean O'Neill almost turned back as snow crunched under his boots.

Coming here to see Courtney was ridiculous. She clearly preferred her independence. Yet his stubbornness—or was it foolishness?—kept him going. He didn't want her to be alone for Christmas. In a few of their talks, she'd let it slip she was single and estranged from her family and friends, and just thinking about that, he ached for her.

Sure enough, his family had noticed and been nudging him to go see her ever since. Especially his brother, Declan. And fine, the chance to see her again was Sean's early Christmas present to himself. Plus, it might be his wishful thinking, but good things had happened to him during the Christmas holidays several times. "Miracles for Christmas," he'd called them.

Was it too much to hope for another miracle this Christmas?

Lord, please guide me. If Courtney is the woman You meant for me, please help me, well, not to mess it up.

His heart shifted as if someone had already stomped on it like he'd been stomping on the snow—or like the one woman he'd fallen for before had stomped on it. He readjusted his scarf as the wind slammed his face. Protecting himself from the wind wasn't difficult. But how could he protect his heart?

Argh. He'd been in this situation before, pining for someone who hadn't returned his feelings, so why was he doing it to himself again? Several women in Cowboy Crossing had hinted they'd love his affections, but his heart had never stuttered in their presence as it did in Courtney's.

Months after meeting the reclusive pilot, he'd expected to get over his crush.

Yet he hadn't. Something about the vulnerability in those eyes as blue as the sky she loved so much got under his skin, along with the hurt she'd done her best to hide. Even the faint scent of her floral perfume—jasmine, maybe?—placed a longing in his heart and kept it there.

He'd occupied himself with tons of work at the ranch where he'd grown up and lived his entire life, but he couldn't forget her. How could anyone? She was so different from anyone he'd met. She'd kept to herself, but that didn't stop him from wanting to get to know her. Of course, he'd had to respect her boundaries, so he hadn't made a huge effort. Well, not until now, which was his last chance.

His phone rang, and he fished it out of his coat pocket. "Hello, Declan."

"Just wanted to make sure you're still on the way to see Courtney." Declan sounded as cheerful as always.

"Yes, I am. But remind me again—Why did I let you talk me into this?" Sean's heart shifted. Would Courtney be glad to see him? Or send him on his way?

"Because I'm an awesome brother." Declan's lighthearted teasing contrasted the tension knotting up inside Sean. "And because you *wanted* to be talked into this."

"This will be my last attempt to ask her out, though." Sean's rib cage tightened as he saw her place. The lights were on. She was home. "I'll let it go after this. I'll have to."

"Or she'll say yes, and you both will live happily ever after," the optimistic world traveler said.

"Yeah, right. I'm not putting my hopes up past a simple conversation." His steps slowing, Sean took a deep breath of frosty air for courage and readjusted the fragile flowers of winter jasmine in his hands. Was this too forward?

"Remember, confidence is the key. Especially when it's combined with kindness."

"Maybe bringing a bouquet wasn't a good idea." For the first time in his life, Sean wished he had suave skills with the ladies like his player brother Declan, who to everyone's surprise had recently fallen in love and gotten married.

In fact, Sean was the only one from their family of cowboy brothers who was still unattached. "The last fortress standing," he'd joked before, but the joke hid some bitterness he hoped no one caught.

"I wouldn't give you bad advice, would I?" Declan chuckled.

"Okay, I'm about to knock on her door." Sean climbed up her porch. "I'll call you later."

"You'd better." Declan disconnected.

Sean swallowed hard, then knocked on the navy front door. Unlike most homes in Cowboy Crossing, this one on the outskirts of Springfield didn't have a wreath. For so many days, he'd thought about all the things he was going to tell her. Yet now all the words hovered on the tip of his tongue and then disappeared like his breath in the frosty air. It was too late to turn around, though.

Huh.

Nothing happened. Nobody opened the door, but based on the lights, she must be home. His heart sank onto the tawny doormat that teased him with "Welcome." Apparently, he wasn't welcome here. Did she not want to see him?

Declan would say she could be in the shower or simply didn't hear him. Sean knocked again. And again.

No answer, and that was an answer in itself. He was wrong about not getting his hopes up, and now those hopes were crushed like snowflakes under his boots.

The only thing left to do was to turn around and go home.

He did turn around. Then a weird sound reached him from inside the house. He whirled back, trying to place the sound. It wasn't like someone was saying something. It was more like—a groan, maybe?

He moved closer to the door and listened. "Courtney, are you inside? Are you okay?"

Had she slipped and fallen and couldn't get up? Maybe on the ladder while decorating a Christmas tree? His stomach clenched as he knocked again, louder this time. He called her phone number and received long beeps, but the ringtone played just inside the house. It stopped ringing once his call went to voicemail. He tried again with the same result.

He glanced at her neighbors' dark windows. He obviously couldn't ask them when they'd last seen Courtney.

"Courtney, are you okay?" he yelled, alarm ringing inside him. Somewhere in a tree, a bird took flight with a protest, and there seemed to come a disappointed meow from that direction. But no sounds from the house filtered through the front door again.

Neighbors' cameras might record him if he tried to enter Courtney's place, and neighbors could report him for unlawful entry. But Courtney's well-being was more important.

He tried the door handle, and it gave in. That was usually a bad sign, and he flinched. The door could be open because she'd forgotten to lock it—that was what Declan would say. But the realist in Sean suspected it could be a burglary in progress. The wise decision would be to call 911 and wait. But worry spurred him on.

His senses on high alert, he turned the handle and rushed inside.

"Courtney, are you home?" He kicked off his boots so as not to trail in snow.

The first thing he saw was the festive Christmas tree blinking its multicolored lights and an apple-red ornament smashed nearby on the carpet, as if it had been crushed underfoot. The second thing... He gasped as he rushed to the motionless body on the carpet, her leg at a weird angle, and blood trickling down from her lip.

Chapter Two

Every bit of him went cold. But as much as his every cell screamed at him to help her, he needed to make sure whoever had beaten her up wasn't still in the house. Sean would be no use to her if he got knocked out.

His pulse thundering in his temples, he dropped the winter jasmine bouquet and cleared the rooms one by one. The tiny place only had one bedroom and one minuscule bathroom, so it didn't take much time. Though every second felt like an eternity when Courtney was lying there, helpless, injured, or... *worse*.

He shuddered as he dropped to his knees near her on the beige living room carpet, the cheery blinking lights mocking the situation. He didn't even want to think what that *worse* could be. "Can you hear me? Courtney!"

No answer and no movement on her part.

"Courtney!" He pulled his phone out of his pocket with trembling fingers and pressed 911.

As he listened to the beeps, he took her hand carefully in case a bone there might be damaged and probed for a pulse, praying as he'd never prayed before.

Please! Please!

Air whooshed out of his lungs when he distinguished a weak one. Yes!

"What's your emergency?" A female voice came on the line as if speaking from another world.

A part of him was in shock, but this wasn't the time to go into an emotional stupor.

As he explained the emergency to the dispatcher, the rational part of his brain cataloged her injuries. "She's not responsive, but there's a weak pulse. Her lip's split. Her hair's matted with blood. Her nose is smashed to the side. I–I hope it's not broken. Some swelling near her eye promises soon to be a nasty bruise. Her leg is crooked at a weird angle as if... as if broken."

Everything inside him shattered. Who could've done this and why?

"We'll dispatch an ambulance and the police. Please don't move her. It can exacerbate her injuries."

"Understood. The injuries like... like the spinal cord." Oh no. He hoped with all his heart that her spinal cord wasn't damaged.

"Keep her comfortable and clear the path for paramedics. What's the address?"

He gave the address and after a few more questions disconnected.

As he brought her a blanket, a thought struck him. The trickle of blood from her lip was fresh, and the bruise hadn't set in yet. If he'd come in a little earlier, he could've stopped whoever had done this.

With such injuries, she could be bleeding internally with possible damage to her organs. His fingers fisted around the blanket, and he resisted the urge to drop it and hit the wall. A riotous heat surged in his veins. If he found whoever had done this...

Droplets of sweat dampened his forehead. He discarded his black coat and white scarf on the nearest chair and knelt near her again, then spread the soft blanket over her, praying and praying and praying again.

Growing up, he and his brothers had gotten into some mischief, earning plenty of scratches and bruises, but never anything like this. Lead coiled in the pit of his stomach, but he had to keep moving for Courtney's sake.

The place was scarcely furnished, so he only had to move a coffee table out of the paramedics' way. Then he dashed into the kitchen for something to help reduce the swelling on her face. He picked a bag of frozen carrots from the freezer and wrapped it in a kitchen towel with a cheery cartoonish airplane on it.

Back near her again, he pressed the improvised ice pack to her bruised cheek. "Courtney, can you hear me? It's going to be all right. Help is on the way. It's going to be all right." He needed to believe the latter himself.

He pushed a clump of matted chocolate-brown hair away from her face, his fingers connecting with her smooth skin. He'd dreamed of touching her. But not like this.

Never like this.

Her eyelashes fluttered, giving him hope, and then her eyes opened in a tiny slit. Her gaze was unfocused.

"It's me, Sean. An ambulance is on the way." He wanted to gather her in his arms, to keep her protected from harm, but doing so could harm her instead. "It's going to be all right," he said for the third time as if that could help make it true.

Sirens wailed in the distance, singing out perhaps the sweetest of all sounds. Her bloodied lips moved, but no sound accompanied it, and her gaze remained unfocused, which wasn't a good sign.

Was she even aware he was there or what was happening? "Can you see me? Stay with me, please. Stay with me. Please. Please!"

A lonely tear slipped from her eye and disappeared on the thick carpet. His eyes burned with unshed tears he had to keep at bay.

At the knock at the door, he jumped to his feet and rushed to open it to paramedics. Cold air gushed in with two young women in paramedic uniforms, then a police officer.

Sean explained the situation as succinctly as he could. The paramedics started with vital signs, then hoisted Courtney on a gurney.

The police officer stepped to him and introduced himself, though the name didn't filter through the overwhelming worry. "We'll need your name and your relation to the victim."

Sean flinched at the word *victim*. "I'm Sean O'Neill. I'm…" He stumbled. Who was he in relation to Courtney? He wasn't her boyfriend or even a friend, really. He'd offered her friendship, but she'd never taken him up on it. "A guy with a crush on her" didn't sound right.

"I'm an acquaintance." He jerked after the paramedics who were rushing to the door with Courtney strapped to a gurney, but the police officer stopped him with a gesture.

The guy raised an eyebrow. "Did Ms. Rogers say who caused the injuries?"

"She didn't regain consciousness long enough. Listen, I–I need to go to the hospital with her."

"I understand. But don't you want us to find who did this to your… acquaintance? May we see your ID?"

"Of course, I do!" Sean deflated. He showed the officer his ID.

"What were you doing this far from home, Mr. O'Neill?"

An engine noise receded as the ambulance drove off. Sean suppressed irritation. "I came to ask her to dinner or maybe even invite her to spend the holidays together. I met her some time ago, and I like her a lot. She wasn't looking for romance, but I was hoping that might change. Holidays and all."

"What about picking up a phone, you know?" The cop's eyes narrowed. "Doesn't everyone text these days?"

Sean resisted the urge to grind his teeth. "I wanted to do it in person."

"You admitted she rejected you before. You could've lost self-control after she rejected you again."

Sean jerked back a step. The guy couldn't be serious! "Why would I call it in, then?"

The officer shrugged. "Some people have their conscience wake up at an inopportune time. And some people think calling the crime in makes them look innocent."

Sean reined in his emotions. Starting to shout would only prove the policeman's point. And he needed to get to the hospital as soon as possible. "I'd never hurt someone. The neighbors' cameras might've recorded something. Why don't you check them? Or talk to Courtney when she regains consciousness."

"We intend to." The officer nodded. "You can go for now."

Sean was near his rusty-trusty truck before he realized he'd forgotten his coat and scarf. But he didn't run back, so he just cranked up the heat.

He requested the GPS give the address of the nearest hospital. Being nobody to Courtney would complicate matters there, as well. He wasn't authorized even to get an update on how she was.

But the main thing was for her to survive.

Chapter Three

Courtney floated somewhere, and the current wanted to pull her under.

But the police officer's question torpedoed her to the surface. The rough voice seemed to be floating somewhere in the fog. Her left eye was swollen so much she couldn't open it, so she squinted her good eye at him and did her best to focus on the words, even if his shiny buttons and clean-shaven face with a square chin still seemed to float somewhere. His head was shaved, as well, and he looked like a famous actor, though she didn't remember which one. But the head wasn't as shiny as his buttons. He smelled of coffee and a hamburger. With lots of onions.

Did she like onions?

Focus! It was important to concentrate on the question.

What was he asking her?

Oh, right.

"My ex-husband... beat... beat me up. Lowell Heller. He was abusive... during marriage. But never... never like this." Every word came at a cost. Her lower lip was split, and her swollen tongue felt as heavy as a log in her mouth. A wet log. Because her mouth was wet. Though why would it be swollen? Her tongue was one of the few things Lowell couldn't hit.

She slid her tongue along her teeth. At least her teeth were there. All thirty-two of them, she hoped, and she stopped counting after ten. Or... "How many... teeth people have?" she whispered.

"Thirty-two." The police officer looked at her as if doubting her reliability.

Lowell had told her nobody would believe her if she reported her injuries. That he'd just make it worse for her. As a CEO of a successful company, he had such a great reputation. The only unfortunate thing about him was that his wife was a compulsive liar.

She can't be blamed, poor thing. She just mixes things up.

Like now. What was that actor's name?

She shuddered and tried to look around to make sure he wasn't here already. Thankfully, only machines and the police officer were here. But he was frowning. Maybe he'd asked her something again. The painkillers the doctor prescribed must be doing their job a little too well. "Excuse me?"

"Do you have an address for him? And a phone number?" The police officer raised his voice.

"He moved... abroad. Don't know where. Didn't... want to know. Changed... his... phone number." Not that she'd want to contact him, anyway.

"What was the argument about?"

"That I left him. But he wouldn't need an argument. I guess he didn't want me to spend Christmas without his signature present." Alarm flashed through her. Some of the words he'd said needled her. That he had... something. But the cocktail of drugs in her system was probably too much to recall for sure.

Not that she wanted to remember, anyway.

After a few questions, the doctor showed up and sent her into merciful oblivion again.

Then it was not so merciful. The nightmare with Lowell made her thrash and scream, which sent a sharp pain to her lungs. The medical personnel rushed in and injected her with something.

Sometime later came a scent that oddly comforted her. It was a welcome and nonthreatening addition to the antiseptic odor. Some kind of cologne and maybe leather. Or hay?

Maybe she'd imagined the scent because it was something safe to hold onto. Like she'd seen Sean O'Neill in her dreams after her nightmare, heard his voice telling her everything was going to be all right. Of course, it was just her imagination because he was miles away and nothing was *ever* going to be all right. She'd be better off to remember she wasn't safe. She was never going to be.

The dreams changed, but the scent of hay and leather never went away, wrapping her like a warm, soft blanket. The voice was somehow connected to a blanket, too. Sometimes a coffee aroma intermingled, but the first scent stayed.

Then another fragrance joined it. Pine needles.

Like a Christmas tree? Why would there be a Christmas tree in her hospital room?

After some time, she didn't want to float out of the sleep or oblivion or whatever this was, but her throat felt dry as a desert. And she needed to know the extent of her injuries. She couldn't move her leg, and that injected panic into her. Was her leg still there? She'd rather lose a few teeth than a leg. She had thirty-two teeth and only two legs.

She opened her good eye and blinked.

Was she still dreaming? Sean was sitting by her bed, his cowboy hat pushed back, his expression worried. On the window behind him, a branch of a fir tree held a sparkling silver ornament, and the rest was wrapped in a silver garland. There was a source for the pine-needle smell. But she felt anything but holiday spirit.

"Oh good. You're awake. I'll call the nurse." He brightened.

"Wait. Water," she whispered.

"Oh yes, right." He placed a straw in a glass and brought it to her lips. "The doc okayed it for me to give you a drink."

She managed several tiny sips, then larger ones. "You're here." Her voice was weaker than she wanted. But then, everything about her was now much weaker than she wanted. Her gaze moved to her legs, and she exhaled. Her right leg was dressed in a cast, but it was there.

"Yes." He smiled sheepishly. "I'm here."

She didn't phrase that right with her mind so sluggish. Forming a thought was like trying to make a linebacker move. Well, one who didn't want to move. Not that she'd ever tried. She'd just watched football games because of Lowell. *Stop.* What was she going to ask? "*Why* are you here?"

"I came to... to visit you. Then I found you unconscious." His eyes darkened. "I'd give most of my life to be there sooner. Thanks to your testimony and your neighbors' cameras, I'm no longer a suspect. But it still took a lot of persuading to be allowed into your room."

Even her sluggish mind recognized the simple truth. "You saved me." Why had he come to visit her, though? After her divorce, she'd become as prickly as a porcupine. No one visited porcupines, right?

"I wish I was there earlier." A muscle moved in his jaw.

A young nurse with a sandy-blonde French braid and snowman-patterned scrubs walked into the room to check the IV, then smiled at Courtney. Her snowflake-shaped earrings danced in her ears when she moved her head. "You're awake. Good. I'll let the doctor know."

The doctor, a short woman in her midfifties, tucked bobbed salt-and-pepper hair behind her ears as she peered at Courtney with kind gray eyes. "I'm Dr. Gilmore. Ms. Rogers, we went over your injuries with you before, but I believe you're better equipped to discuss them now. We ran CAT scans and X-rays and did blood work. As you no doubt already noticed, you have a broken leg and broken ribs—two of those to be precise."

Courtney gasped. "Two broken legs?"

"No. Two broken ribs."

"Oh, okay. I guess only two out of twenty isn't that bad. Or how many ribs do people have?" Uh-oh. Hopefully, the good doctor wouldn't think they needed to stop her painkillers immediately.

Dr. Gilmore and Sean exchanged glances, and then Dr. Gilmore cleared her throat. "Twenty-four. Thankfully, the broken ribs didn't puncture your lungs. But you also were bleeding internally from a ruptured spleen."

"That's bad. Only one spleen." Courtney clammed her mouth. She really needed to keep quiet. She usually knew well how to keep quiet. Her childhood survival had depended on her ability to be quiet.

"The scan suggests there wasn't any damage to your brain." Huh. The good doctor didn't sound so sure about the latter. "Thankfully, your nose was fine, though we initially suspected it could be broken. You also have various cuts and bruises."

"Oh. I'd better not ask for a mirror, right?" Courtney's hand moved to her face and touched her cheek, which must be black and blue by now, not to mention swollen.

She *felt* the bruises before, though not nearly as much as usual thanks to the meds. But before the doctor mentioned them, she hadn't considered how horrible they must look. Her gaze moved to Sean, and she resisted the urge to lift her hand to cover her face. How ridiculous. She'd just been told about a ruptured spleen and broken bones, and she worried about how she looked in front of Sean?

He touched her hand, then jerked his away as if he'd done something he shouldn't have. "You still look beautiful. I mean, it's not that I think bruises are beautiful. They are awful. But you don't look awful." He stumbled, and a mottled red blotched his neck. "I mean—I should let the doctor speak."

"Good idea." Dr. Gilmore nodded. "We repaired the ruptured spleen and stopped the internal bleeding. We had to reset the broken bone in your leg, so you'll need to be in the cast for six weeks. We're keeping your cuts disinfected."

"Thank you," Courtney whispered. She had the weird feeling the doctor was talking about someone else lying in the hospital bed. Because despite the pain, a part of her still didn't want to believe it was her, didn't want to believe Lowell could do this to her again even after she'd fled him. After she'd been on her own for some time.

Hadn't such naïveté gotten her in this situation to start with? Even when the violence started escalating, she hadn't wanted to believe the man she loved and who'd promised to spend his life loving her could hurt her.

People couldn't be trusted. Her gaze moved from the doctor to the man near the hospital bed. Even people like Sean.

Dr. Gilmore's eyes hardened. "There's nothing we can do about broken ribs, though the good news is they didn't puncture the lung, tear the aorta, or lacerate your kidneys or liver, though as I said your spleen suffered damage. Some movements will hurt until the ribs heal. Laughter will, as well."

Courtney rolled her eyes. Well, her good eye, that was. "I don't intend to laugh anytime soon. Probably not ever."

"Don't say that." Sean's fingers brushed against her hand, then moved away fast. The touch was fleeting, and yet she felt it all the way to her heart.

Why was she reacting to him this much? Irritation fissured her already broken heart. She gave him *the look*, but it might've been only half-efficient with one eye. "Even my smile must look like a grimace right now."

"It doesn't." He moved closer, bringing that scent of leather and hay that made her hold on. "It looks nice. Better than nice."

"*Suuuuure.*" She scowled to prove her point. Was he here with her this whole time? But why? Did he feel sorry for her?

She lifted her chin. She didn't want people to feel sorry for her. She'd worked hard to build an independent life for herself. "When can I start flying again?"

"Flying?" Dr. Gilmore raised an eyebrow.

"She's a pilot," Sean supplied before Courtney could.

"I can answer the questions." Courtney threw the words in his direction. Lowell had always spoken for her, too. It had taken her so much effort to be able to voice her opinion. She couldn't ever risk losing her voice again. As raspy as it was right now.

"Of course, you can. I didn't mean to..." The admiration in his eyes dimmed, causing something inside her to dim as well. "Right."

But didn't the porcupine stick their needles even in those they didn't want to hurt? Simply because someone got too close? "I have clients who've booked flights."

"Not until the cast is off. And you'll need a lot of rest. I'll prescribe some painkillers, and you'll need to make an appointment with your primary doctor soon to ensure everything is healing nicely. We'll keep you for observation for today, but we need to discuss your care after discharge." Dr. Gilmore flipped a page on her clipboard, her shortly clipped fingernails without polish as no-nonsense as the rest of her was. "You'll be requiring some care at home. Do you have someone to help you?"

"No," Courtney said.

"Yes," Sean said at the same time.

"Look, I live alone. I don't even have a cat." It wouldn't be fair to a pet because she often had to fly a jet at the drop of a hat, and no, the rhyme didn't make her smile. "I doubt my plants can help care for me." And her sister and mother... they didn't speak to her anymore. Courtney had kept people at arm's length, so she couldn't exactly call her colleagues for help now after having pushed them away. "I'll manage."

"You don't have to." Sean's eyes met hers and held.

She narrowed her good eye, but his gaze didn't waver. A wave of awareness passed through her battered body.

"I'll leave you two to discuss this." The doctor's voice softened. "We can help set up home health nurse visits. But we can't release you from the hospital without releasing you into someone's care."

"Thank you for the information, Dr. Gilmore," Courtney said, and then the doctor left.

Instead of relaxing in gratitude, Courtney's stomach clenched. She was not only battered but also helpless again, and with every fiber of her being, she hated the feeling.

She pinned him with a stare of her good eye. Maybe she should've requested an eye patch, a bandanna, a striped shirt, and black pants instead of a hospital gown. Then she could pretend to be a pirate. "Why are you doing this?"

Based on his neck movement, he swallowed hard. "Because you need help and I can provide it."

"Don't you have a busy job?" Her mind whirled, trying to find a solution to her dilemma. She had acquaintances in different parts of the country, but she wasn't close enough—physically or emotionally—to call and ask them to drop everything and fly here to take care of her.

"I work with my brothers, and we help each other. And it's the least busy season on the ranch. I mean, we still have work, but not as much as in summer."

She'd never had anything like that sense of a community helping each other. Her sister and she had cared about each other at first, but neither of them wanted to be a punching bag and preferred to ensure the other one took the punches. Sadness stirred her, but she had much more important things to be sad about. It could be worse. Lowell could've killed her.

She shuddered. Then a memory of another loss filtered through, so horrible it made her struggle to breathe. Something far more tragic and painful than beatings or broken bones had occurred in her life. She'd lost something beyond precious, and she still couldn't even think about it. The biggest tragedy of her life, and it was all her fault. Tears burned her eyes, but she didn't deserve the respite from crying.

Though she didn't want to remember Lowell's recent visit, a part of her needed to. He'd said something important. But what was it? The memory of his boot hitting her made her shudder again.

Sean's gaze became concerned. "Are you cold? Would you like me to ask for an extra blanket?"

"No. It's not that."

"Well, if you don't trust me, I can get you references."

It wasn't a chuckle, but some weird sound passed her throat. The doctor was right because the pain did reverberate in Courtney's side. The pain-med cocktail must be wearing out. "No, it's not that, either. I know Declan well enough. And he said great things about you." She paused. "Why were you in the area?"

"I wanted to ask you out. To dinner. Maybe even Christmas dinner. Maybe even... even to celebrate the holidays together."

Her insides warmed.

Seriously? What was wrong with her? Well, besides the obvious.

Didn't she know it wouldn't be right to lead him on? How could she put this delicately without offending him? Despite being cold to him, she felt certain vibes. "I–I know you like me a little."

"You do?" The blush on his neck deepened. "I mean, you know... not that you like... Just, you know..." He frowned. "I so wish I was better with words."

And on some level she didn't want to admit, this rugged cowboy appealed to her. The open gaze of his brown eyes. The five-o'clock shadow on his face—How long had he been here, exactly? And would it be rough to her touch?

What was she thinking? Heat flared inside.

She couldn't help liking the way he jumped to her rescue. The way he still cared even after she'd given him the cold shoulder. And speaking of shoulder—those broad shoulders were nice to look at and should be even better to lean on. Another wave of awareness went through her. But he definitely, totally, absolutely didn't need to know that.

"Your words are not the problem here," she whispered. Her voice sounded raspy again, as if unused for a long time, like her sense of optimism. "*I'm* the problem here."

He shook his head, nearly knocking his brown cowboy hat off. "You're not the problem!"

"Please." Courtney lifted her hand with the IV needle stuck in it. "It's difficult for me...." She took a deep breath. That malty-brown gaze tugged at her, but she had to be firm. "I was broken inside already, and now I'm physically broken in many places. I'm just trying to survive. I'm not looking for romance. I can't afford romance. I can't even move yet."

"I understand. And I'm so sorry for everything that happened to you. If I could meet your ex and exchange a few words—" Then his eyes widened, and he jerked back. "You didn't think I was trying to take advantage of the situation, did you?"

"No. I just wanted you to know." She looked away. She didn't want him to see her as a victim.

He seemed like a great guy who deserved someone better than her. Someone whole, not broken, for starters. Now her heart ached more than the rest of her body.

"Listen, if you think I'd be taking you home to my place and putting you in an awkward situation of living with me, it's nothing like that. I live on a ranch. One of my brothers lives nearby with his family in a large lodge. It has plenty of spare rooms, and each room locks with a key. It's behind a tall and massive security gate. Made from cement. Well, it looks like pretty stucco." He stumbled. "Well, you get the idea."

She did. Lowell's heart was made of cement but with a pretty stucco-like façade. Sean's suggestion also gave her an easy excuse. "I wouldn't want to intrude on your brother."

"See, my brother and his wife and their two children are leaving today for a three-week Christmas vacation in France and Germany. I talked to them, and they'd love to have me and you to house-sit for them." He searched her face as if she'd be doing him a favor if she agreed to stay at the lodge instead of the other way around. "That's the beautiful part I think God arranged just for this."

"Did God arrange for me to get beaten up, too?" She regretted the words the moment they slipped off her tongue.

His expression stilled. He pulled off his hat and twisted it in his hands, his knuckles flexing and whitening beneath the pressure as he focused on them. "I don't understand why bad things happen. But I hope God will make something good come out of this. My parents are excited to have you come, too. They are staying at the lodge this week as they have the bathroom renovated at their ranch house, but it's almost done. Declan and his wife would love for you to join us for the holidays, too. Genevieve said she still can't thank you enough for saving her daughter. My entire family would love to have you."

Seriously? She stared at him again. "Just like that?"

Sean beamed. "You don't know my family. And I can't wait for you to meet Ada. She can be unfriendly at first sometimes, but I assure you she's lovely. I adore her."

Unexpected jealousy speared her—or was it her rib? "Who's Ada?"

The one that was so lovely. The one he adored.

Courtney shifted in her bed, and the machine beeped as if protesting, as well. Ada couldn't be his girlfriend, right? Because he wouldn't be admitting that he liked her, Courtney Rogers, and would be offering to introduce her. Or...

"Wait a second. I'll show you her photo." He reached for his wallet.

Her heart sank. "She must be very important to you if you have her photo in your wallet."

"Well, it's the photo of us together." He pulled out a photo from his wallet.

"Of course. It's the photo of you together," Courtney said drier than she'd intended. She had no right to feel jealous. And really, in her condition, why did she worry if Sean had a girlfriend? It would be a shocker if he didn't have one, a handsome, caring, hardworking guy like him.

He was a catch, and she could admit it, even if she wasn't interested in romance.

She swallowed hard, reluctant to look at the photo. He'd probably be hugging that woman, too.

He placed the photo in front of her. Well, he did have his arms wrapped around... a dog.

She blinked. Was her eyesight going down like her other organs? "Um, where is Ada?"

"Well, right there." He pointed at the photo.

She blinked several times again and squinted. Nope, same photo. "I only see you and a dog."

He sent her a worried glance. "Ada is the dog. A beauty. I named her Ada because it means noble in German—and she's a noble German shepherd." Worry appeared in his eyes. "Are you okay with dogs?"

A dog! Yes! "Totally." It was people she sometimes had problems with. "Do you, um, have a girlfriend?" And why did she hold her breath waiting for the answer? Why was the answer so important to her?

"Because, you know, then she might not like a female living in the same house as you. Even with separate rooms, each with its own lock. Unless I was a dog." She cringed. What was she saying, seriously? "Which I'm not." And why on earth did she need to clarify *that*?

"I'm single. No girlfriend." Then his grin slipped. "I doubt you'll like Scratcher, though."

"Scratcher?" she echoed, surprised by how relieved she was that he didn't have a girlfriend.

"My mom's cat. Let's just say, he lives up to his name."

She rolled her one good eye again. "What's a few scratches added to the collection I already have?"

He scooted closer, his eyes going tender. "Does that mean you agree? And I promise to keep the cat away from you."

"No! I mean, not about the cat. About staying at the lodge." A shiver ran over her spine. "And I don't know when my ex might show up again for fresh vengeance."

His jaw set tight. "All the more reason to come to the lodge. My brothers with families live nearby at the ranch, and I can stay at the lodge for some time. You'll have your separate quarters and your privacy, I promise. My brothers and I have rifles. My parents, too. One of my brothers is a cop and his wife, too. Another brother is ex-military."

"Not to mention, there's a scary cat." Any other time, her lips would curve up.

"That's right. We'll protect you."

It would be so easy to say yes. But she couldn't. Unshed tears prickled her eyes.

The young blonde nurse came in. "Ms. Rogers, you need to rest."

If only she could.

Chapter Four

"Are you comfortable? Are you okay?" The next day, Sean glanced back before returning his attention to the country road. Due to the cast and the need to keep her leg stretched, she'd taken the truck's back seat. At least, he sure hoped it wasn't because she didn't want to see him.

"I'm fine. Thank you. And it's the hundredth time you've asked." Then Courtney's voice softened. "Though I do appreciate it."

"You're welcome. It's probably only the *ninety-sixth* time I've asked, but good point." His fingers tightened around the steering wheel's smooth surface.

One would think he'd feel less tense once back in his hometown, on his home turf, so to speak. Especially compared to the desperate intensity of the hospital. Or was it *intense desperation*? Unlike Declan, Sean wasn't great with words.

Yet nerves were still getting the best of him. He raked his fingers through his hair. "I hope you'll like it here. Or did I say that a hundred times already, as well?"

"No. Only ninety-six." It wasn't a chuckle, but when he glanced back at her, the corners of her split lip curved up.

Not laughter, but he'd take it. His spirits lifted as he looked at the gravel road. Besides, laughter would literally be hurting her.

How could her ex-husband do this? Heat surged in Sean's veins again, and his fingers nearly fisted. He bottled it up and let the hills covered with sparkling snow and spotted with cows and horses comfort him, the scene so familiar. While she traveled the country and likely the world as a pilot, this was the place he loved. The place where he belonged.

Where did she belong? He didn't know, but he was eager for it to be someplace secure.

He sniffed the air, hoping he'd aired out the scent of fried onions from the recent takeout. Her signature scent of jasmine seemed to fill the space, and just that aroma made his heart beat faster.

"My family is super friendly. We tease each other sometimes. But we do it with love." He meant it.

His heart constricted, the lump heavy in his chest. She'd been upfront with him about not looking for romance, and he respected that. So his heart needed to slow down in such proximity to her. He'd have to suppress his attraction. It was the right thing to do.

He was a simple man with everyday wishes. He got up at dawn, worked hard, and loved the land he'd grown up on and the creatures God put on it. Sean didn't question much. He'd never had to. But now he couldn't understand how such a horrible thing could happen to Courtney. No, he didn't know her well, but he knew she didn't deserve it. No person did.

A myriad of emotions whirled inside him now like snowflakes in a blizzard. Anger, compassion, hope, longing, and many more he couldn't identify or maybe didn't want to. They were slipping away just like snowflakes, as well, and new ones appearing. He just knew his world had turned upside down and his life had changed when he'd found her bleeding on that carpet.

Well, his life had changed the moment he'd met her, but he hadn't realized it then.

"I just hope the sight of me won't scare them." Her voice in the back seat hardened.

He winced. "No! And you look wonderful." He stumbled. "Okay, not that you look wonderful with bruises." How did he walk into that trap all over again? "And they'll heal soon."

"True, but I don't think I'll ever heal inside." Her voice dipped lower, and he barely heard it above his truck's motor.

"I pray you will." In fact, he said a prayer right now. With the bright cerulean sky ahead and the sunshine bathing the beautiful winter wonderland, so pristine, it was difficult to believe the hurt she'd endured was possible. But it was already imprinted on her body and soul.

"I stopped praying a long time ago," she said.

This was another reason they couldn't be together, as if he needed to add more to the list. The lump in his chest clenched tighter. How could his heart even beat when constricted like that?

"I don't want you to pity me." Her voice barely traveled over the seats.

He wished she was sitting near him. Not only because he could hear her better then but also because he wanted to see her expressions. Even better would be to see her eyes. He swallowed hard.

Maybe it was for the better. He needed to concentrate on the road. While there was little traffic here, a horse could jump the fence or something. It had happened to one of his sisters-in-law and just happened to be his brother's horse, bringing them together as his brother tried to make up for the escaping horse.

Sean knew how his brother felt. Sean wanted Courtney to be safe. He wanted her to be safe always.

He almost said he had compassion for her and not pity and that it was different. But he stopped himself. He drew a lungful of fresh country air as he lowered the window a slit. "I don't pity you. I admire you."

"Huh?" Her incredulous voice warbled. "You *admire* me?"

"It takes a lot of courage to be a pilot. Frankly, I'm trembling before I board a plane, and I'm just a passenger with little responsibility." It was foolish to admit his fears when he wanted to look heroic.

"I got scared at first, too. I couldn't believe I could do it. But now I'm thrilled when I'm in the air." Her voice grew louder, strengthening with her passion.

"It takes a lot of knowledge, as well. I can't imagine seeing all those things on the dashboard and knowing what they are for. You must be very smart." He slowed around a curve. He wasn't just buttering her up. He meant every word.

While he found her attractive, with those expressive blue eyes, lovely features, and long chocolate-brown hair, more than her physical appearance stirred his soul. He didn't see her as someone weak and helpless, but as someone who'd gone through horrible things and instead of giving up had rebuilt her life brick by brick. While other people complained about mundane struggles, she'd gone through so much more without a single complaint.

How could one not admire a person like that?

"Right." She snorted. "If I were smart, I wouldn't have married a man who made a punching bag out of me."

He ground his teeth against the injustice of it all. "Don't blame yourself for what he did. He's a horrible person. But horrible people can be charismatic at first, pretending to be nice and kind."

Uh-oh. He sent a glance back before looking at the winding road again. Hopefully, she wouldn't think *he* was pretending to be nice and kind to trap her.

"I should've seen through it, though. And there were signs. Anger flare-ups at other people when he didn't like what they said or did. He said I should support him, and I naïvely believed those other people were wrong and he was right. Then his silent treatment when he didn't like something *I* said or did. Or what my friends or family said or did. I had to earn his approval again. And I craved it so much that I did my best. Then—well, you don't need to hear my sorry story."

"I do." He ached to take her hand for comfort, to do something to help her. But all he could do was listen and grind his teeth.

"No, you really don't. I guess it's right what they say. When one wears rose-tinted glasses, all red flags are just flags. Or what do you call it? The boiled-frog syndrome."

His curiosity piqued, he glanced at her in the rearview mirror. "What is the boiled-frog syndrome?" Was it something about French cuisine? But he doubted she'd mention it then.

"Basically, if the frog jumps into the boiling water, it will jump right out and survive. If the water is just warm when the frog jumps in and the temperature is gradually increased, the frog will get... well, boiled."

"Oh, wow. You know about psychology then." He whistled.

"It's a rather popular concept." But her voice initially lifted as if she liked the praise, then hardened again midway through as if she remembered that liking praise had gotten her into the proverbial hot water to start with.

He eased up on the gas pedal as the familiar hill and its large fence appeared in the distance.

Usually, that sight calmed him, but today apprehension tightened around his rib cage. He inputted the code, and the gate slid open.

"We'll give you access to the app that controls the gate. As well as access to all the cameras inside and outside the house."

Before Sean even parked, Declan rolled out the wheelchair, his newlywed wife by his side. Ada shot out of the house and ran to the car, barking loudly.

Sean parked and turned off the engine. It'd be easier to talk without the motor growling alongside the dog, though he wasn't sure what to say. "We already had a ramp installed for my parents here, in case they need it for the future. In the ranch house, too. So that was another point in staying here."

"I could make it up the steps on crutches. But it's a good thing I don't have to."

He got out, walked around, and opened the truck door. Ada rushed to him, barking happily.

"I'm glad to see you, too. Missed you!" Sean petted his dog, then held firm when Ada growled at Courtney. "That's a friend. Her name is Courtney. And from now on, you're to protect her, as well."

Ada sniffed the air, then side-eyed the newcomer, but settled on the snow, perhaps understanding the message for now.

"Good girl." Sean gave her a quick back rub, grateful the German shepherd didn't bare her sharp teeth at Courtney any longer. "Stay." Then he turned to Courtney. "You already know Declan and his wife."

"Great to see you again, Genevieve. I'm glad this is under better circumstances. Hello, Declan," Courtney said. "Thank you so much for your hospitality."

The rest replied with pleasantries.

Yup. Something shifted in him. Courtney *would* think being beaten up and needing caring support was better circumstances than when she'd flown them in a desperate search for Genevieve's missing daughter. He leaned to Courtney. "I'll help you move into the wheelchair."

She waved him off with the bouquet she'd insisted on picking up on the way from the hospital, along with a box of chocolates. "I can do this."

He took the flowers and chocolates for now. After a few grunts, she slid into the wheelchair.

"We're glad you're here, though we wish these circumstances were different, as well." Genevieve leaned down to hug her, clearly careful not to further damage those broken ribs.

Sean had a feeling that if these circumstances *were* different, Courtney wouldn't have shown up at the lodge. But he kept that to himself. And yes, he'd desperately wanted to see her again, but he'd rather spend a lifetime without seeing her than have her hurt.

"Thank you." She smiled, but it was a bit strained at the edges. Or maybe it seemed that way because her lip hadn't healed yet.

"Welcome! Welcome! Welcome!" Accompanied by his father and thankfully not by Scratcher, his mother rushed down the stairs, carrying a pumpkin pie and adding its sweet aroma to the frosty air.

Ada looked up at the pie with hope, so Sean spoke in a stern voice. "Stay."

The dog looked away as if to say, "I didn't want it much, anyway." Then, in her noble pose, she froze in place like a statue.

Then Mom's eyes widened when she saw Courtney's battered face. Her bright, open smile faltered before she recovered fast, and the grin bunched up her cheeks again. "Welcome, Ms. Rogers. We're happy to have you here."

He looked down at Courtney as he handed back the flowers and chocolates to give to the person who was the present boss of the house here. Well, besides Scratcher, of course.

Courtney's small smile stayed in place, probably with a great effort, but the sadness in her blue eyes showed she'd noticed the momentary lapse. She handed Mom the roses and chocolates, but since Mom's hands were occupied, Dad accepted them. "Thank you very much. I hope I'm not intruding."

"Not at all. We *luuuuv* having guests. Especially now that nearly all my sons have flown the coop and started their own families." Mom lifted the pie. "Don't get scared. I'm not going to make you eat an entire pie right here. It's just a symbol of hospitality and a sign of more to come."

"I appreciate it." Courtney's cheeks gained some rosy hue after being pale in the hospital, and her smile looked more natural. Maybe another time, she'd have laughed. One could hope. "And I happen to love pumpkin pie."

He rolled the wheelchair up the ramp, and Dad held the front door for them. Declan lifted Courtney's suitcase from the car, and Genevieve snatched up the crutches.

Inside, the rustic-chic lodge smelled of pies and his mother's signature beef stew. The scent of home to him, even if it wasn't his childhood ranch house. But what would it feel like to Courtney?

His family had done all the preparations for Courtney's arrival. He couldn't even help with information because every time he asked Courtney what she liked, she answered first with "everything," then with "it doesn't matter."

Thankfully, Scratcher was nowhere to be seen, and for the first time in a long time, Sean was grateful to the cat. Of course, the feline would appear to reestablish his authority soon enough.

Sean pushed Courtney's wheelchair into the living room, his cowboy boots echoing against the hardwood oak floor. Mom and Dad had rolled up the usual rugs that depicted untamed wildlife. They probably worried the wheelchair would catch on them, but those critters still yowled and prowled in the paintings as if decrying that they were kept from the cozy fireplaces.

He helped Courtney out of her bright-blue parka, then took off his coat. Once everyone shed their outer clothing and boots, Mom asked, "Would you like the yellow room or pink room or blue room?"

Wow. Of course, her foresight shouldn't surprise him. Still, Sean could've hugged her for preparing three rooms instead of one, though based on Courtney's blue jeans and a navy turtleneck sweater she wouldn't be picking a yellow or pink room.

"That's very kind of you to give me a choice. The yellow room, please." Courtney's voice softened. "It sounds like sunshine."

Compassion flashed in Mom's eyes. Clearly, if it were up to her, she'd gather this wounded bird under her wing. "It sure does."

"Stay," he told Ada as she trotted toward the yellow guest room, her nails clicking against the hardwood. The German shepherd sat outside the room, motionless like a statue again.

Scratcher seemed to be hiding still. Despite the popular saying, Ada and Scratcher got along well enough by leaving each other alone. It must help that Mom gave her cat extra love while staying here. Ada had wisely stayed away from the cat, not questioning his authority.

Sean rolled Courtney into a room with terracotta-hued walls and sturdy oak furniture that must've served for decades. But the canary-yellow linens and throw pillows added a splash of sunshine, as did the chair upholstered with mustard-yellow fabric. Oil still lifes hung in descending sizes on one wall, each depicting yellow roses or tulips or carnations. A pine bough with gleaming golden Christmas ornaments emanated a subtle spicy aroma from the nightstand, and right near it, candies, including lemon drops, filled a gold-rimmed glass vase to the brim.

"I don't know how to thank you." Courtney lifted her eyes at Sean, then his mom, dad, brother, and sister-in-law.

"You already did. Many times." Mom waved her off. "We all just want you to get better. Oh, and please feel free to use anything in this room and bathroom. My daughter-in-law already left some exotic-smelling shampoos and soaps she brought from Asia. I added more toiletries with jasmine and jojoba."

"I'll be glad to pay you for them. As well as for the stay and food." Courtney touched the pine bough, her gaze pensive.

"Well!" Mom gasped and pressed her hand to her chest. Her voice rose an octave. "Now you're offending us!"

Ada growled from the hall, but then went silent. Maybe she understood it was a false alarm.

As Courtney's eyes dulled, her hand shot up as if to defend herself. "I didn't intend to."

His gut knotted, and he stepped forward.

But Mom's smile softened already, and she waved away Courtney's apology. "Pshaw, no worries. I'll let you get settled. Then please join us for dinner. I understand you're tired, so I can bring it to your room if you want me to. But we'd love to have you join us if you're up to it."

"Thank you. Um, will the wheelchair make it into the bathroom?" Courtney's gaze traveled to the door. "Or, um, maybe I can just hop there."

They all looked at the door and then at each other as they realized the dilemma. He'd ordered a smaller motorized wheelchair that would be easier to maneuver, but it wouldn't arrive until tomorrow.

Then he had an idea. He wasn't an impulsive man, but he acted on it before he could chicken out. He swept her up and carried her into the bathroom.

She gasped. "You... can't be doing this."

"I think I just did." He was shocked himself.

Her eyes went wide. From up close, he could see darker specks in them. Her fast breathing feathered against his skin, and that made his breathing go shallow. He gathered her a little closer, enjoying the feeling of her in his arms and the subtle fragrance of her flowery perfume—jasmine, right?—more than he should. His heartbeat skyrocketed.

Did she have the same reaction? No, that was just wishful thinking. She'd made her stance loud and clear before. Yet it didn't ruin the incredible moment of having her close, of holding her, of looking into her eyes.

"You can put me down," she whispered.

Hmm, yes, but where? "I, um, don't want you to just be standing on one leg like a crane, holding onto walls. Not that cranes hold onto walls." Yup, Ada would be a better conversationalist than he was. Scratcher, for that matter, too. The cat always got his point across when he didn't like someone, which was most of the time.

"Um, on the edge of the bathtub is fine," she said, perhaps reading his thoughts.

"Right." He sure hoped she couldn't read his *other* thoughts.

He placed her on the tub, though that couldn't be comfortable, and moved the shower curtain aside. Its buttery-hued chrysanthemum print danced as if caught in a breeze. The matching bathroom towels and backsplash tiles gave the room a cheerful feel.

"I could've made it here on my crutches." She lifted her chin.

"Right." He nodded.

She cleared her throat. "That means I'll need them to make it back."

"Right." He cringed. What could be more awkward than saying the same word three times in a row? He sounded like a parrot, and not even one with extensive vocabulary. "Let me bring them."

He rushed back into the room where the welcoming committee had dissipated probably to give Courtney privacy. Something he should've done, as well. He clattered the crutches together and brought them to the bathroom that smelled of jojoba shampoo.

Then he leaned them against the wall within easy reach. "Here we go. Do you need anything else? Maybe the bag with your toiletries?" Did her shampoo smell of jasmine like her perfume? And why did the mere thought send his heart racing?

Maybe inviting her here wasn't a good idea. He could barely fight his feelings for her already, and he'd always worn his heart on the sleeve of his Wrangler's shirt. She'd see right through him. On the contrary, she kept her heart hidden behind iron walls. Probably three rows of them.

The corners of her battered lips curved slightly. "Your mom kindly left all the toiletries I need here. Way more, actually. And it's going to be a challenge to take a shower with a cast."

"Right." Well, well, well. He just answered his question. More awkward saying the same word three times in a row was doing it *four* times in a row. "Should I bring you some cellophane wrap or something to keep the cast from getting wet?"

"Thanks. I'll figure it out after dinner."

"Ri—okay." Heat crept up his neck when he realized she was waiting for him to leave. In a small consolation, at least he didn't say "right" again. He backed out of the bathroom, nearly knocking the crutches down, and the heat spread from his neck to his ears.

"Wish I could figure out this courtship thing," he whispered to Ada as he leaned and patted her in the hall. Her short black-and-brown fur felt smooth under his hand.

Ada lifted her head, then barked twice. She might've given him some solid advice. Or she might've just been hungry. In case it was the latter, he checked on her bowls and filled one with kibble and the other one with fresh water. Ada started munching on kibble.

The clattering of pans reached him from the kitchen. He might as well make himself useful, so he strode there. He and his brothers had shared duties while growing up, so he knew his way around the kitchen. Okay, he couldn't yet replicate his mother's Irish beef stew, despite having the recipe, but then, none of them could.

"What can I help with?" he asked his brother.

"We've got everything covered already. The table is almost set. By the way, awesome romantic move by carrying Courtney." Declan winked, then retrieved a lemonade pitcher from the refrigerator. "You're learning."

Sean swallowed hard. "On the contrary, I've made more mishaps in the last two hours than in my entire life."

"Really?" Declan laughed. "You must have a faulty memory." Teasing was abundant in their family, but Declan was the biggest jokester of all. The class clown, too. It was a mystery how he'd married an English teacher who was a bookworm by her own admission.

"Be supportive." Genevieve nudged him in the forearm.

The oven chimed in, and Declan snatched the mitten before Sean could. "Let me get this, darling." So much love shone in his eyes as he looked at his wife.

That look wrapped longing around Sean's heart and squeezed it painfully. He was thrilled to see all his brothers fall in love and get married because it made them happy and he loved seeing them happy. Plus, it made their parents happy, which was important. Being single hadn't bothered him much before.

But after meeting Courtney, a significant part of him longed to have what his brothers and their wives had. Losing his heart to a woman who had zero interest in having it made the longing so much deeper.

Time to refocus. "I'll take Ada for a walk after dinner, but did anyone take her out earlier?"

"I did. Okay, I hope I won't sound like a hypocrite. But what I'm going to say might not be so supportive, though." Genevieve plucked biscuits from the tray and plopped them into the bread basket, and the aroma of freshly baked goods made his stomach grumble. "A lot of women would find the gesture romantic, yes. But some women in this situation might think you view them as helpless."

"I just didn't want her to struggle." He carried the pitcher and the bread basket to the dining room and set it on the table beside a gigantic bowl with the stew still bubbling hot.

Genevieve followed him with napkins and tucked them under the utensils. Small earrings in the shape of books moved in her ears as she did. "We understand and admire that, and I hope she does, as well."

Scratcher ventured into the kitchen and lapped up some water, then sat, and stared at Sean in open contempt, expressing disapproval over him bringing another person into the house. Sean knew better than to pick up the cat and try to pet him.

Then he nodded toward the living room. "I'll bring the Christmas tree tomorrow. Without Scratcher here, it's going to be easier for Christmas ornaments to stay on the tree. So grateful Mom agreed to let us use lots of our decorations here."

The cat hissed as if to say he did what he wanted whenever he wanted, and the humans should've learned that rule by now.

"Mom wants Courtney to feel special. But I'm afraid she's getting up her hopes of something between you and Courtney." Declan winked at Sean again while carrying a large salad bowl.

"Oh no!" Sean groaned and unstacked the plates from the end of the table, dishing them out to everyone's places. "I don't want Mom to get upset later. There's nothing between me and Courtney. There can't be."

The knock of crutches on the oak floor announced Courtney's arrival, and if he hadn't still been carrying two plates, he'd have slapped himself on the forehead. Not good timing for him to have said those words.

If she'd heard what he'd said, she didn't show it. Her expression was neutral. "This looks and smells wonderful." Though she could've used the wheelchair as there was enough space to make it through the bedroom door, she clearly preferred crutches.

Her navy turtleneck hugged her nicely, and the color made her blue eyes stand out even more. Her long hair, gathered before in a low ponytail, now flowed over her shoulders, and the sapphire earrings dangling from her ears sparkled and matched her sweater. She was a sight to be seen, and he couldn't look away.

A nudge from Declan warned Sean he was staring. Thankfully, he didn't wink this time.

"Mom's beef stew is very much in demand in our family and this small town." Sean pulled out the chair for her. "Does your leg need to be elevated?"

"It's going to be all right like this." Her expression tensed, and she probably clenched her teeth as she sat. She must be still hurting. Most likely, she would be for a while.

Based on the sound of Ada's toenails, she walked into the living room. She knew well not to go to the dining room. Scratcher knew it, too, but he didn't obey the rules and was currently washing in a corner.

Mom and Dad strolled into the dining room, holding hands after many decades of marriage. Their example was the reason it had taken him and his brothers so long to get married. All of them wanted that special forever bond their parents had.

Including Sean.

Once everyone was seated, Mom said, "Let's pray."

Courtney's eyes darkened, but she didn't protest. Then she bowed her head and took Sean's hand on one side and Genevieve's on the other. As the simple touch affected him, he did his best to calm his rapid heartbeat.

She didn't echo everyone's amen after his father had said a prayer. Going through so much hurt without the comfort of prayers must've been a million times more difficult.

"Thank you for including me in the prayer," Courtney said quietly.

"Of course." As was the tradition, Mom ladled the beef stew for everyone, and they passed bowls down the table. "I hope you'll like it. It's a traditional Irish dish."

"I have no doubt I will." Courtney's smile was warm.

After everyone had their first fill, she raised her head. "I'm sorry to say I can't stay long. One or two days maximum, and I shouldn't even do that."

What? His spoon dropped into his bowl, splashing stew onto the oak table.

She continued looking straight ahead at no one in particular. "Sean said he shared my story."

"Yes," everyone else responded in unison.

The delicious, hearty food soured in his stomach. This was all his fault. "Is it because I've been crowding your space too much? I can be... less hovering. I won't be a helicopter..." He searched for the right word because the usual one for this expression obviously didn't fit here. If the cat sat in the corner by his choice, Sean had managed to get himself there with his words by accident. "Helicopter... friend, I guess."

Scratcher either licked his paw or covered his eyes with it from second-hand embarrassment for Sean. Sean suspected it was the latter. Then the cat meowed, probably joining Ada in giving Sean solid dating advice that sadly Sean couldn't understand.

"It's not because of you. And I happen to like helicopters. And planes, of course." She glanced into his eyes before facing his mother. "And not because I don't like it here—I love it. You're all amazing. But I might be bringing danger to your doorstep. Coming here at all was selfish of me." Her battered mouth set in a determined line. "I do need to leave as soon as possible."

Pain sliced him. He dabbed up the stew splashes and fisted his soiled napkin into a wad. He worried about her, but as she'd also pointed out, he'd put his parents in danger.

"Nonsense." Mom waved her off. "We'll have none of that leaving thing. First, we already discussed it as a family, and we all voted to bring you here. My husband and I are going back to our house after dinner. We were only staying here because of the bathroom renovation, but the boys finished it this afternoon. So you're not endangering us at all."

Sean sent his mother a grateful glance. He should've better explained already, but his brain turned to mush in Courtney's presence. "Second," he broke in, "I talked to my brother Cormac—he's former military, by the way. He's offered to monitor the camera feed inside and outside, excluding your room, of course. He checked everything before you moved in. Oh, and he'll move in if needed and if you're okay with it. All the rooms have locks for privacy—I said that already, right?" He hesitated. "If it's okay with you, I'd like to text him to watch the camera feed."

Courtney nodded. "It's kind of him to volunteer to do it. But I'd rather he didn't move in."

Taking that as an okay for Cormac to watch the camera feed, he texted him and received a simple reply with "Sure."

Scratcher seemed to think he'd bestowed humans with his presence long enough and walked out of the room.

Genevieve raised her hand like a student, instead of the teacher she was, asking for permission to speak. "Third, there's more to this lodge than meets the eye. It's truly a modern-day fortress. My foster sisters and I decided to get it for protection purposes. We had it renovated to withstand the assault of a brigade. It was... it was precautions to protect my daughter—and well, you already know how that turned out. But she'd have been safe if she'd stayed here. In addition to the cameras and extensive security system, we have a secret safe room downstairs that blocks off the rest of the world. Plus, it has a secure storehouse of ammunition. Even the windows are bulletproof. Thankfully, my daughter is no longer in danger. But the precautions are still here. Ready to be used, if needed."

"Wow." Courtney's eyes widened. "Sean told me this was 'like a fortress,' but I thought he was exaggerating to encourage me to agree."

He leaned toward her, everything in him hoping she'd change her mind and stay. Not just for his sake, though there was that, but also for hers. "If anything, I didn't say enough. My older brother is a cop. He'll patrol the vicinity from time to time, especially at night. All of my brothers are trained in firearms, as are all of my sisters-in-law, though some of them are more comfortable with weapons than others."

"I'm the least comfortable one." Genevieve raised her hand again. "And my combat skills are limited to, well, falling on someone. But my foster sisters could teach your ex-husband a valuable lesson or two."

He winced. Courtney had permitted him to explain what happened to her, but he didn't want her to hear the reminder. Not that the pain was likely to let her forget it any time soon.

Genevieve planted both hands on the table, and her hazel eyes narrowed above full cheeks. "Any of them would be willing to move back here to help you if needed. However, one of them would be coming with a baby, so that might not be ideal. I'd offer to move in, as well, but my teenage daughter is home on vacation. And sadly, I'd be the least useful to you."

A racket deep inside the house made them flinch, and Sean leaped to his feet while Courtney paled. Her hands fisted and rose to her chest.

"What's happening?" He drew his gun. "The alarm would've gone off if someone managed to breach the fence or break inside."

"And Cormac and Ada would've warned us of anything suspicious." Declan followed him to the source of the noise while Dad went to get his rifle.

"Right." Sean nodded. Must be his new favorite word. Why wasn't Ada barking?

Okay, now she did bark, but it wasn't a warning bark, more like scolding someone.

They rushed into what Mom would've called the pink room and found the German shepherd standing near a shattered flamingo-pink vase with watermelon-flavored chewy candies in pink wraps strewn on the floor.

Scratcher was sitting on the nightstand, making a good substitution for the vase and hissing at the dog. Then the light-gray cat looked at them and stretched his neck toward poor Ada. Sean could almost imagine the naughty critter saying, "Look, the dog did it. Thankfully, I arrived in time to warn you."

Ada looked up with a bewildered look, then whined. Maybe the cat and the dog didn't get along as well as he'd thought they did. Either way, the cat was going home soon where he could rule the house the way he wanted.

Tension easing out of him, Sean chuckled as he scooped up candies to throw away.

Declan wiggled his finger at the cat. "I think we know what happened here."

The cat raised his head and blinked gleaming green eyes, probably appalled that someone didn't believe his innocence.

Everyone else filed in. Mom raised her phone. "I just checked the camera footage. Yup, Scratcher did what Scratcher does." She scratched behind the cat's ears, and he purred.

Sean gave some love to Ada to make it fair. "You did good." Then he whispered in her ear again. "But best stay away from the cat and his shenanigans next time, right?"

As Ada barked in response, he caught Courtney's gaze across the room. Color returned to her face, and her lips raised into a quarter smile. He'd take it.

As they settled at the table again, he faced her. "I believe this is the safest place on earth for you."

It didn't matter that her being here wasn't safe for his heart. And he couldn't exactly keep her here wrapped in a cocoon—he wouldn't do it if he could. As she'd said, she needed to fly, and a bird like her flew in high skies.

Still, his protective instincts flared up. How was he going to protect her when she ventured out to town? Or when she eventually left?

Most likely leaving him with a broken heart, though his broken heart mattered much less than her life.

Chapter Five

The next day, Courtney breathed in the frosty air as she sat in a backyard surrounded by a tall fence.

She was wearing one brown boot trimmed with cozy faux fur, and Sean had wrapped her leg cast in cellophane, supposedly to protect it from the snow. The cloudless sky spread on forever with a beckoning lazuline blue tint, and she wanted to be there, away from the earth and all the problems.

Far, far away.

She looked at the Christmas lights in the shape of a snowman, then at Ada, who ran around for some time, and now settled on the snow in front of Courtney. Then her gaze moved to Sean. "You don't have to stick around with me. I can get inside on my own."

"I like being around you." Ducking his head, he rubbed the back of his neck. Then peered up at her with a sheepish smile. "Is there anything you'd prefer to do right now?"

His smile tugged at her. He'd shaved his beard and mustache. Today, he wore a knit beanie instead of the cowboy hat he usually carried around, and yet he was still movie-star handsome. She'd watch the movie if he played the hero.

Uh-oh. What was she thinking? She couldn't fall into the same trap she'd spent years clawing herself out of.

She looked away. "This is the perfect weather to go skiing, but I can't with a cast." She chuckled in a somewhat bitter sound as she swept away more snow from the bench she was sitting on. Then she gestured to the Christmas light figure. "I can't even build a snowman because my crutches might sink into the snow. And no, I don't need you to carry me around."

She'd never wanted to be a burden. Especially now. But then, while she might not be great company, she could still do a lot of things. She picked up the Frisbee and whirled it into the air. "Ada, fetch!"

The magnificent dog ran, muscles playing under black-and-brown fur, then went airborne, caught the Frisbee, and brought it back. She dropped it at Courtney's feet proudly. The German shepherd seemed to be warming up to her, and that softened her heart.

"Good job." She rubbed the dog's back and gave her a dog treat. Ada's wet nose touched Courtney's palm as the German shepherd nuzzled for her treat. Then Courtney sent the Frisbee flying again. After ten more times, she set the Frisbee aside.

"Well, how about we play snowballs?" Sean scooped up some snow, already starting to make one. Ada tilted her head, perhaps wondering what he was doing. "I must warn you, though. My brothers and I had plenty of snowball fights when we were children."

"Seriously?" Couldn't he see it? Did she have to spell it out for him? She gawked. "Um, I can't run or hide." Including from Lowell. If she hadn't disappeared to this lodge, would he have come back and finished what he started?

Most likely.

The frosty air seemed to freeze inside her lungs, protected by ribs. All twenty-four of them. The police still couldn't find Lowell's whereabouts, and she didn't expect them to.

"You can duck." Sean shrugged. "There's a way for everything."

"Hmm." Of course, he'd go easy on her, even if she didn't want him to.

When she'd left Lowell, she had started over from zero. With her self-esteem beaten into dust, she'd promised herself she wasn't going to concentrate on the things she couldn't do. Besides, her broken leg was temporary, while so many people lived with disabilities their entire lives.

He was suggesting a fun game, not for her to shovel snow from the driveway to the street like she'd watched him accomplish this morning.

"Why not?" She gathered snow into her mitten. "Let's do this."

He walked the distance to the looking-like-stucco fence but didn't try to hide behind the nearest tree with branches covered generously in a white coat.

Under Ada's curious watch, Courtney balled up the snow near her feet and lined up a row of snowballs on the bench.

"I never had snowball fights as a child," she said, though Sean probably couldn't hear her from that distance. "But I do have a good aim."

So did her ex. She winced and pushed his image out of her mind. At least, for now.

"Ready?" Sean grinned. He had such a wonderful smile. Sincere and open, it seemed to make the snow around him sparkle and the snowman grin.

She shouldn't be noticing that. At all. "Sure." She threw the first snowball and missed. Mostly because Ada jumped in the air and caught it in her teeth.

"Ada, no!" She couldn't help smiling at Ada's bewildered expression as the snow started melting in her mouth before she placed the snowball at Courtney's feet. "We don't want you to get a cold." Dogs did get colds, right? Courtney or her sister had never been allowed to have a puppy. Even a goldfish, for that matter.

"Ada, stay!" His voice was stern.

The German shepherd plopped on the snow. Courtney petted her so the dog wouldn't get upset about something that wasn't her fault. "You did good. It's just a different game, and you don't know its rules yet." Just like Courtney had never been able to figure out the rules of the games Lowell had been playing.

Sean threw a snowball in response, but he didn't aim at her because it landed way to the left. Ada moved her head, following the trajectory, but didn't jump to catch it this time.

"Good girl. You're learning. Some things should be let go." A lesson Courtney needed to remember herself. Her heart shifting, she rubbed Ada's smooth fur again.

The large dog turned away from her as if saying, "Well, you didn't catch it, either."

Courtney almost chuckled. *Almost*. She wiggled a finger at Sean. "You can do better than that!" She wasn't some fragile crystal vase he needed to be careful with or fear shattering. "Let me show you how it's done." Her snowball splatted on his shoulder.

He laughed without even trying to brush off the white powder. "Game on!"

This time, she had to duck as white snow hit the house wall behind her. "Finally!"

Ada growled at the snowball embedded on the wall now, then pushed one toward Courtney with her nose.

"Thank you for your help, Ada." Courtney sent several snowballs back, one grazing his forearm and another one hitting him in the chest. "Look and learn!"

Sean laughed, the sound reverberating inside her. "Not bad at all!"

Ada waved her tail proudly, and Courtney petted her again. "You helped a lot!" Well, mostly by staying out of the way, but Ada didn't need to know that. "Yes, you did."

By the time they were done, Courtney was laughing, and the doctor was right, it was painful. She doubled down, hugging her middle and her aching sides.

His features twisting, Sean was by her side in a moment. "Are you okay? Did I hurt you?"

Ada whined as she jumped and trotted toward Courtney, then licked her face, her tongue rough against Courtney's skin.

"No!" She looked up at him. "I mean, I'm okay. Well, more or less. And no, you didn't hurt me. I was laughing because I had fun. And these broken ribs do hurt when I laugh."

He winced. "I'm sorry."

"Don't be. I had more fun than I remember in years. Maybe, except when I'm in the sky, but then I have to concentrate and pay attention." After years of fearing doing something wrong, then wincing from every sound suggesting Lowell had found her, she could just relax. Let it go. If only for a few minutes.

His expression became unreadable. "I can't help you take a plane into the sky. But maybe I could do at least something."

She was about to say that she didn't need him to do anything at all, but curiosity won over. "Like what?"

Ada tilted her head again, obviously curious, as well.

He stepped closer. "Did your father or uncle ever play airplane with you when you were little?"

Courtney stifled a snort. "The best I could hope for from my father was that he wouldn't find me when I was hiding." Her red-mittened hand flew to her mouth. She shouldn't have said that. She'd learned to keep her past hidden after she'd told Lowell and he'd used it to his advantage.

Sean's eyes darkened. Then he exhaled a puff of humid air that lingered in a frosty cloud. "Want to try now?"

The idea sounded ridiculous. And a little scary in the sense of being so close to him. But then, she'd spent such a big part of her life being afraid of her own shadow, scared to try new things, to try anything at all.

Then she could've died on that carpet near a Christmas tree if Sean hadn't shown up. Life could be so short. Besides, he had a point. She didn't need to be able to walk to play airplane.

She pulled her shoulders back and said again, "Why not?"

"Why not, indeed." He turned around.

At first, he simply gave her a piggyback ride along the backyard, and she held onto him. Then she spread her arms, imitating airplane wings while he held her and whirled her around.

She even growled a little. "Rrrrr."

Ada looked at her, confused, because clearly *she* was the one who was supposed to growl when needed. Then she howled her response as she ran around them, thankfully, without tripping Sean.

It brought a smile to Courtney's face. "Rrrrr. That was the sound of the engine. Sort of." She nearly chuckled before she remembered her broken ribs and pushed it back.

Of course, there was no comparison to flying, but her chest still swelled, letting in a pleasant feeling that even her broken ribs, her broken self couldn't poke into and burst.

"Did you like it?"

When he placed her on the bench again, she had to stop herself from reaching out to him. She didn't want her eyes to say too much, so she leaned to Ada and hugged her. When Courtney knew she'd composed herself, she looked up. "I did. Thank you."

He beamed as if she'd awarded him with some special prize. Then his smile slipped away. "Are you cold? I should've asked already. How about some hot cocoa with marshmallows?" As Ada jumped at the word *marshmallows*, he added. "No cocoa for you, but there'll be a dog-appropriate treat."

Ada seemed to be fine with that because she climbed the steps to the house fast. He opened the door and commanded, "Stay." He wouldn't want wet paw prints all over the place.

Hmm. The dog wasn't the only one with wet paws. Courtney hadn't noticed her snow-wet mittens until now, but her hands were getting cold. She raised her scarf to cover her chin, then glanced at the cerulean sky, wanting to stay. But heading inside was wiser. If laughter made her sides hurt, she didn't want to imagine what a cough would do.

She reached for her crutches. "Hot cocoa with marshmallows sounds awesome."

"Great." He brightened. "Would it be okay if I carry you inside instead of you navigating the porch steps again?" While the front entrance had a ramp, the back entrance had three steps.

"That sounds reasonable—" She was about to continue with a *but*.

He didn't wait for the second part of her sentence as he scooped her up. "Okay, then."

Was it too late to protest?

No, it wasn't. But she couldn't make a sound as he carried her three steps up onto the porch and then inside the warm house. Just like the first time, the gesture stole her breath away. Yesterday, he'd taken her by surprise. Besides, the wonderful feeling of being in his arms had been overshadowed by the embarrassment of needing help to get to the bathroom, her nervousness about meeting his family, *and* her irritation over a macho move that didn't consider her opinion. Unlike Lowell, who hadn't seemed to care about her opinion, Sean had no doubt meant well, but the irritation had still twisted her gut.

This time was different. He'd asked permission. And maybe it was the surprisingly good day she'd had outdoors after being stuck in the hospital bed. But her heart started beating erratically, and a pleasant wave—part delight, part excitement, part am-I-really-doing-this swept her up. Like the first time she flew solo. She even wrapped her arms around his neck, though she completely, totally, absolutely shouldn't have.

When he put her down, a sting of regret over the short distance suggested her initial spark of attraction toward him was growing. She'd better extinguish it fast. "Thanks. But you shouldn't do that again."

Immediately, she ached to take those words back as her entire being begged to be in his arms again. But she'd best not give into this feeling. She took a deep breath of air scented with pine needles and his scent of hay and leather. Not helping.

Ada whined nearby, likely feeling something was wrong but not understanding what exactly.

His eyes dimmed. "Understood. I'll bring in your crutches." The motorized wheelchair he'd ordered for her had arrived today, but she preferred to keep moving on crutches. Maybe she needed that sliver of independence, or maybe she'd been punishing herself. She didn't want to analyze that.

Great. She'd sounded ungrateful when he'd done so much for her. But it was best for them both not to fall in love. "Um, is that towel for cleaning Ada's paws? Is it okay if I do it?" The need to be useful flared up again, embedded from childhood when she'd only get bits of parental love if she were useful.

"Yes, it is. Yes, if you don't mind. I'll bathe her after we get cocoa."

The dog eyed Courtney as Courtney lowered herself to her knees, her cast clunky and uncomfortable. "Well, Ada, let's try to do it. If I'm, um, too rough or something, please let me know. By barking, not biting, okay?"

The German shepherd lifted one paw but didn't make any promises.

By the time he brought the crutches, Ada was running around with relatively clean paws, and Courtney had taken off her mittens and shrugged out of her blue parka and red stocking cap.

He accepted them and tucked them in the crook of his arm. "I'll get your mittens dried." Then he grasped her hands. "Your hands are cold." He blew on them and rubbed them. "Better now?"

"Y–yes." Her pulse went wild again.

If he did something like that when she'd been hooked up to the heart monitor in the hospital, it would start beeping loudly, and the nurse would run inside.

He winked. "And a cup of hot cocoa should help, too."

"Yes. Certainly." She already felt hot inside, and not from thinking about the hot cocoa. She hadn't felt this way since she'd met Lowell.

The thought had the effect of a cold shower on her. Or rather as if a snowball the size of a snowman's head had hit her. She staggered back.

"Let's get to it then. I'll meet you in the kitchen." He strode to the mudroom to hang their coats, and Ada trotted after him.

Her earlier exhilaration diminished, Courtney wobbled into the kitchen, the crutches clattering against the hardwood floor. He still made it there before she did and had already given Ada a treat and fresh water. Then he washed his hands with liquid soap, the scent of oranges spreading in the kitchen, and she did the same afterward while he warmed water for the cocoa in the microwave.

He placed a mug with hot water on the marbled-gray counter as she perched on a tall stool, then dropped onto one knee, sending her heart into a somersault. "I forgot about the cellophane. I'll unwrap it, okay?"

Of course. He was on one knee to unwrap the cellophane. He didn't even touch her, and yet an unfamiliar fleeting feeling went through her. The feeling of being cared about. That was why it was unfamiliar. Well, she'd thought Lowell had cared about her, but it'd all been an illusion.

"I appreciate it." She poured the cocoa powder and stirred with a candy cane. The wonderful aroma spread in the room.

"We can sit in the living room if you want to." He slid the marshmallow bag toward her. "As children, we fought over who got the most marshmallows. Now we can have as many as we want."

Huh. He talked a lot about his childhood. No wonder, as it seemed as warm and sweet as this drink. She wasn't sure she wanted to remember hers. No, wrong. She was sure she didn't want to.

"I'm fine here. Let's stay." She added marshmallows without counting, then tested a careful sip. It warmed her inside, or maybe Sean's caring gaze was what warmed her as he sipped his drink. She turned away because she couldn't allow herself to care in return.

"Would you like to join me in decorating the Christmas tree?" His voice made her look up.

"Hmm. I wondered about the tree that miraculously appeared in the living room this morning," she muttered, drinking some more of her cocoa.

His chest puffed. "Not miraculously. Declan and I dragged it in."

Then the image of the small Christmas tree in her living room this year, her feeble attempt at normalcy, intruded. It was the last thing she'd seen before losing consciousness. That and Lowell's heavy boots. Those she didn't just see. Felt, too.

She winced and nearly dropped the mug. She clattered it onto the counter to avoid shattering it like her heart.

"Did I say something wrong?" He set his mug beside hers, one lonely marshmallow floating there.

"No. Not at all." She used to have a heart as soft as that marshmallow. But not any longer.

A part of her wanted to coil into a fetal position to protect her vital organs—she hadn't done a good job the last time, and her spleen had paid for it. Another part of her wanted to run.

But if she did either, she'd let people like her father or Lowell win. And it wasn't like she had something better to do with all the time she'd unexpectedly gotten on her hands. She'd never been one for social media, and while she appreciated the stacks of romance novels by Autumn Macarthur and Jessie Gussman that Genevieve had given her, Courtney didn't feel like reading about romance these days.

She couldn't offer to clean or shovel snow from the driveway—Sean had shoveled it this morning anyway. Yes, she'd watched him too long from her window.

Her cooking skills left a lot to be desired, at least according to her father and Lowell, and other than maybe repairing tractors or other such equipment, she'd have no clue what to do at the ranch. Decorating a tree, she could easily do, and she needed to be needed, not to be indebted to this family so much.

She'd still leave an envelope with cash before leaving, of course.

"Let's decorate the tree." She straightened her spine to its full capacity and said the phrase she seemed to favor lately. "After all, why not?"

"Awesome. I'll bring the decorations." The corners of his lips kicked up, making him look like a child about to open their gift boxes. But he wasn't a child. He was a muscular, attractive man who—for some reason she couldn't understand—was kind to her. What an intoxicating combination.

But hadn't she once allowed such an intoxicating combination to poison her veins and paid a high price for it? Granted, Lowell had only *pretended* to be kind, but still...

She wobbled on her crutches to the large tree towering beneath the open-beamed ceiling, and the pine-needle scent intensified. Hot cocoa and pine needles. It already smelled like Christmas here, throwing her back into the few happy times of her childhood when she could forget reality.

He brought a chair for her, then placed a stack of boxes on the floor. "If you get tired, just let me know."

Irritation flared. "I'm not going to get exhausted decorating a tree! Even children can do it."

Oops. She winced.

Here we go again, porcupine.

She touched the fir branches. The invisible needles protecting her soft core were much longer than these.

"I'm just saying you're recovering. Or might get uncomfortable standing on one leg. Or... Never mind. How about you do the lower branches while I do the higher ones?" He opened a box with sparkling silvery garlands, then another one with tissue-wrapped treasures.

"Okay." She braced her crutches aside and lowered herself onto the rolling office chair he'd brought.

He strung a gingerbread-man-shaped ornament on his index finger, jangling it. "Cormac brought this one when he was stationed in Germany. They have amazing Christmas markets there."

She selected a purple glass ornament the shape of a butterfly and hooked it on a nearby branch, then tapped it, setting it aflutter. Glitter sparkled on it. "What about this one?"

"Oh, Mom bought it because his wife, Paisley, has an affection for butterflies—as does my niece who lives here. You'll find lots of such decorations around this place." He unearthed a globe with stacks of books painted on it.

"Wait!" She lifted her hand like a student knowing the answer. Must've gotten that from Genevieve. "Don't tell me. Let me guess this one. It's because of Genevieve. Because she likes books." Genevieve was wearing funky earrings, each shaped like a book, and the similar earrings and matching bracelet her daughter had worn helped Courtney find the missing girl.

"Bingo." He threaded its string on the tree in a prominent place. "Makes finding presents for Genevieve so easy. We just buy books by her favorite authors, Autumn Macarthur or Jessie Gussman. Well, first we check among ourselves so we don't buy the same titles, and Declan peeks to ensure his wife doesn't have them already."

They were all clearly considerate of each other. A family as close-knit as her white turtleneck. She'd learned to wear turtlenecks long ago because they could hide bruises on her neck.

Longing constricted her heart. What would it feel like to be a part of a group of people like this family? She and her sister and Mom didn't even talk to each other any longer, and it was all Courtney's fault. Until she left Lowell, she hadn't realized how much he'd alienated her from her family, but it was too late. She'd tried to contact them to apologize, but they'd blocked her. Which she deserved. And her father was gone. Lowell had found an excuse to stop her from going to her father's funeral.

A lump formed in her throat. Then she lifted a giraffe with a little loop on its head. "Huh. What about this one? Someone likes giraffes?"

"Um, my sister-in-law who owns this house traveled a lot for her work. She brought this souvenir from Africa. Sorry I don't remember each country. It's a good thing Scratcher's no longer here. Otherwise, I don't think this tree would stay decorated for long. Ada has done well around Christmas trees. Never touched them."

The dog, who stretched out on the living room carpet, looked up at the mention of her name, then, yawning, rested her head back on her paws, signifying her agreement on both statements.

After dangling the giraffe on the tree, Courtney hung up more globes painted with books in a clear tribute to Genevieve, then reached for a kangaroo. "Did she bring this from Australia?"

"Yes, Arianna did." He opened another box. "Before Christmas when we were nine, Dad took us to the store to choose ornaments. Not surprisingly, most of us chose globes with horses painted on them."

"You, too?" She reached into the box and pulled out a globe with a bay horse.

"I brought home the one with a silver bird." He looked somewhere past her. "I liked it. And I, um, needed the bird to feel wanted and welcome, too. Sounds silly, right?"

"No." She picked up the bird ornament and cradled it in her palms as if to warm it up. "No, it doesn't."

Then she blurted out, "I met Lowell two weeks before Christmas. It was the year before I was going to graduate from high school. Mom worked long hours to put food on the table, so she was rarely home. My sister had already graduated high school, started working, and rented a tiny apartment. Often, I was the only one besides Dad at home, so it was getting more and more difficult to escape his ire."

"That's horrible and unfair." Sean moved closer to her.

"I so badly wanted to escape and was so starved for affection. Later, Lowell often joked that he was my Christmas present." Bile rose inside her. She'd believed him then. "And I'd answer that he was the best present I could ever wish for."

The lump in her throat grew.

The best present ever.

She'd kept saying it even when she couldn't mean it, even when wearing bruises and heartache. She'd kept saying it because he'd expected it, because if she hadn't, he'd hit her again. And it would be all her fault because she'd made him angry. It had always been all her fault.

Always.

Especially that one horrible time... She didn't want to remember, and yet she needed to. What she'd lost was so precious, so important, and it was all her fault for agreeing to Lowell's suggestion—well, usually his suggestions were like orders—because she'd been afraid to make him angry. If she'd given birth at the hospital instead of at home, would her baby still be alive? Pain sliced through her.

Lowell's words as he'd beaten her up this time floated to the surface.

I have something you want.

They didn't make sense because he no longer had anything she wanted. But they would make sense if...

She pushed it away. She had to accept what happened to Lark. She had to.

Sean's hand with a paint horse ornament froze midair, and his voice brought her back to the present. "Some people are great at manipulation."

"Yes, they are." And her radar was way off. She touched a white horse ornament, and it swung from side to side. "I was sure he was my knight in shining armor."

"I'm sorry that happened to you."

At his compassion, she looked up, then placed another shiny globe on a branch. "I mean, I grew up with a man who couldn't control his anger. Why didn't I see the signs in Lowell?"

Sean lifted a frog-shaped ornament. "Boiled-frog syndrome?"

She chuckled without mirth. "Boiled-frog syndrome." She found a globe with a caterpillar cut out from it. "This one was for Paisley, right?"

"Yes. I'm always here if you need to talk, you know." He didn't move. Just stood there, looking at her.

She flinched.

I'm always here if you need to talk, you know.

Lowell had told her that as well. One of the many ways he'd reeled her in. She'd been so desperate then for someone to listen, to understand. She'd thought she'd become independent enough, and yet that desperate need to be understood, to be cared about rose to the surface again, nearly choking her.

But even if Sean wasn't like Lowell, her body tensed, remembering the betrayal. Lowell had been such an attentive listener, her place to escape to when her father had gone on another of his rampages. Her refuge.

The best present ever.

"We had to meet in secret because I wasn't of legal age at first. By the time I was, Lowell proposed. I couldn't wait to escape my nightmarish home, but I was truly head over heels for him. So I said yes immediately." She paused to place a few more ornaments.

"That's not surprising."

Yet she should've known better. "After I divorced him, it took a long time to recover. Then I vowed to myself that I'd stand on my own two feet from now on." She patted her cast. "Well, now I stand on one foot and two crutches."

"You'll be running around in no time." He coughed a little. "Walking around, I mean."

"Enough of my sad story." She didn't tell him the saddest part of it. It was too hurtful to share, too hurtful to think about Lark.

I'm sorry, darling. I'm so sorry.

Courtney kept tears at bay and plastered on a smile. "What are these? Something connected with Ireland?" She picked up an emerald-green globe embossed with shamrocks.

"This is from our grandparents. Our ancestors lived in Ireland."

Her family didn't have any ornaments that had passed down through the generations. Her family had few ornaments to start with, and by the time she'd been in fifth grade, nobody had bothered to put up a Christmas tree.

"Christmas is for children," her father used to say.

Sean stepped back from the tree. "It looks beautiful. You've done a great job."

This time, she didn't correct him that a child could do this. Instead, she said, *"We* did."

He glanced at the garlands in the box. "I'll decorate the walls in the hall real quick, if you don't mind."

"Of course, I don't." She didn't say she could still carry garlands while walking on crutches. She did her best to appreciate him being considerate instead of bristling at him possibly thinking she was helpless.

Had Lowell latched onto her because he'd sensed she was weak?

She raised her chin and walked to the living room fireplace decorated with framed photos of the family, plus a few Christmas figurines. They were all laughing and smiling. Her smiles in photos with Lowell were forced for years, and many times before she'd taken a photo, she'd had to cover her bruises with makeup.

Sean joined her soon with a new box. "Would you help me put up stockings, please?"

"Sure." As she hung red stockings on the wall with family members' names, her heart squeezed. There'd be no stocking with her name here, another reminder that she was an outsider.

Then her hand stilled at the next stocking. "Wait a moment. Do I have a namesake in your family?" Was it the name of the girl who lived here and loved butterflies?

Smiling, he shook his head. "That's yours. We all want you to stay here for the holidays. Please."

Grateful tears prickled behind her eyes. She stroked the stocking's plush surface and the raised embroidery of her name. Very touched, indeed. "Thank you."

Lowell hadn't believed in exchanging Christmas gifts. Not that she could buy him anything without his knowledge as he controlled every penny. As he said, "I'm the one who earns it, after all."

She didn't remember her parents ever putting up stockings for them.

Her father hadn't even bought presents for them any longer after fourth grade. Their mother had, and he'd been angry with her for that, making Courtney and her sister feel guilty. Now Courtney understood he'd find a reason to be angry, anyway. Or if there had been none, he'd make one up, as he often had. She and Monica had begged their mother to divorce him. And she finally had. After Courtney had gotten married and talked Lowell into letting her mother move in with them. That was how the first fights started, and Courtney had blamed herself and gone out of her way to make peace. But Lowell hadn't let her mother stay long. Mom moved into Monica's tiny apartment, and Courtney's broken promise to her mother created a further rift between her and her mother and sister.

Would Lowell come after her here? The thought appeared again, despite Sean's arguments about this being a safe place for her, and a shiver tracked down her spine.

She'd tried so hard and had done her best....

Her rib cage tightened as she stretched to hang the stocking that said Courtney. As a young girl, she'd already learned her best so often wasn't enough.

In fact, it never was.

Chapter Six

By day three, Courtney had met several more members of the family, including the married couple, Paisley and Cormac, as well as Sean's sister-in-law, Madeline.

The tall, slim, stunningly beautiful woman looked like a model, like she'd stepped from a fashion magazine. She had a toddler at home and was a former medical examiner who insisted on checking how Courtney was healing, probably because Courtney wasn't keen on going to the local doctor. Courtney had thought it was best not to point out that Madeline had operated on dead people, and Courtney wasn't dead yet.

After Madeline left, Courtney squandered significant time near the mirror. Covering bruises during her marriage, she'd become a skilled makeup artist. Then in her time alone, she hadn't bothered with makeup much. She'd wanted to impress people with her skills, not her looks.

Today, she'd told herself she needed to cover the healing bruises that still decorated her with different shades of blue and yellow. Well, there were some greenish ones there, as well. But she hadn't done it her first day here, and they'd looked way worse then. Fine, she wanted to look beautiful for Sean. Or as pretty as she could, considering the split lip and yellowish skin over the cheekbone.

Was she attracted to him?

Yes.

The answer was simple. She put her brushes back and washed her face with soap that smelled of jojoba, taking the makeup off. Then she toweled her face off, going tougher than needed. She shouldn't try to appeal to him. It was going nowhere.

Besides Ada following Courtney everywhere—other than the restroom, thankfully—the O'Neill family always seemed to have someone in the house with her while Sean worked on the ranch. Maybe to have people available if needed and to stay out of her way the rest of the time, or maybe to protect her. Currently, it seemed to be Paisley's turn. They were all lovely people, but Courtney found herself missing Sean.

As much as she'd fought the feeling, she glanced at her phone way too many times throughout the day, eager to call him, if only to ask him to stop by. Or maybe he wasn't going to show up at all. What did she really expect?

While she didn't want to believe Lowell, she couldn't forget him saying few people would have patience with her. And look at her yesterday. She'd snapped at Sean for carrying her inside the house, even though he'd first asked permission. Then she'd trauma-dumped on him about her past. Her porcupine needles would pop any person's joy bubble.

Her heart sank to the unforgiving cement floor as she slid from under Paisley's truck in the warm garage. When she'd arrived, Paisley had mentioned her truck was making some weird noises, and Courtney had offered to take a look.

While she wasn't an airplane mechanic, she'd learned from the ones who'd serviced the planes she'd flown. And she'd learned about vehicle parts and simple repairs in her teens because helping her father in the garage had been one of the few things that placated him. Well, mostly. She grimaced.

"What? That bad? Don't worry about it. I can take it to a mechanic in town." Paisley looked up from her butterfly-decal-stamped laptop. Sean wasn't kidding. This girl did love butterflies.

"No, it's good. I found the reason for the noise and fixed it." Courtney lined the tools back up on the shelf.

They'd come in handy earlier when she'd worked on a malfunctioning tractor at the ranch, too. She'd repaired two tractors, which had already earned her a lot of praise from the O'Neills. She'd basked in it, but her subconscious had remembered that Lowell had often praised her in the beginning of their relationship to reel her in.

Then she wiped her hands on a rag, checked the camera footage outside the garage on her phone to make sure it was safe, and opened the door from her phone to let the fresh air in. The technology in this house was impressive, or maybe she just didn't know any better. "Would you mind starting it?"

Paisley climbed inside the truck and did so, then turned off the engine, slipped out, and grinned. "No noise anymore. You're brilliant."

The praise touched Courtney, but she shook her head. "It's no biggie. And I heard you're the brilliant one." She closed the garage door and picked up her crutches to clomp inside the house, then hesitated. "Would you like to share a cup of tea with me? Or coffee? Or—"

"I'd love to." Paisley beamed at Courtney as if she were her best friend ever.

Courtney's heart shifted as she hobbled inside, her crutches knocking a drumbeat against the floor. She didn't have any close friends. Lowell had slowly and deliberately alienated her from everyone but him, and after their divorce, she'd been too scared to trust to make new friendships.

"I'll take our cups to the table." Paisley volunteered, which was good because carrying liquid-filled cups and navigating crutches or hopping on one leg weren't a good mix. Then she also brought the apple pie, freshly made and sent by Sean's mother, to the breakfast nook.

Ada met them and trotted to the cute knobby pine table, then stretched in the sunny spot on the floor, not bothering anyone. A remarkable dog. Noble, indeed.

Courtney studied her companion over the top of a warm cup that emanated a mint aroma.

Paisley and her husband were a rather unlikely couple, at least in appearance. Tall with iron muscles, a buzz cut, and an army posture, Cormac wore a serious expression and chose khaki shirts and cargo pants—maybe because he missed his fatigues.

Petite and slightly plump, with a small baby bump, Paisley wore a perennial smile above her vivid salad-green sweater where a yellow puff-print caterpillar crawled over the left sleeve and left a trail in the grassy print across the front. Not surprisingly, the cheerful creature was also always smiling. Paisley's skirt boasted a giant daisy, with the sunny-yellow center starting at the waist and white petals reaching the knees.

That wasn't all. A weird construction with bumblebee receptacles pushed her pink and azure-blue hair back. Courtney had to blink several times when she'd met Paisley to make sure she wasn't imagining things. As was often the case, looks were deceiving. Paisley, a computer programmer with her own ultra-successful company, had started a charity for abused women. So maybe she was hanging out here not only because Sean had asked her to but also because the cause was close to her heart.

Hmm, while the Irish cowboy brothers had been somewhat what Courtney expected them to be, the foster sisters who'd married them were nothing like she'd anticipated.

"Thanks again for repairing my truck. I owe you." Paisley forked some of the apple pie.

Courtney waved off the gratitude. "Nothing to owe. It wasn't super difficult."

Paisley looked at her from under pink-blue bangs. "You're not used to being praised, are you?"

Courtney's hand hoisting a forkful of pie stopped midair, then resumed its journey. "I'm used to expecting that after the praise often comes scolding. That I've done something wrong again. Or that lots of praise can be followed by years of frosty treatment."

"That's unfair." Paisley's headshake sent her bumblebees bobbling. She sipped her tea, and her breath spread more mint aroma in the air. "When I was growing up, children used to pick on me because I was smaller than they were. Somehow, it was still always my fault. I mean, I'm not trying to compare what happened to you with what happened to me. There's no comparison. I just want you to know it's not your fault."

Courtney chewed on sweet-tasting cinnamon apples. "Thanks." What else could she say? She'd never been a talkative one, which wasn't surprising considering any of her attempts to speak up had been hushed, sometimes with blows.

Could she and Paisley ever become friends? They seemed total opposites, and yet Courtney already felt the sense of camaraderie with the cheerful mother-to-be in her fun outfit. No, it was doubtful. Courtney wasn't going to stay here long, anyway.

The beep on her phone made her slide it from her jeans' back pocket and check the screen. It was from the gate, and an alarm went through her. Sean had given her access to answering the security gate when anyone passed, which had floored her because of the amount of trust and tact. But now Lowell's face appeared in her memory, and she winced as if waiting for a punch.

She pressed the button to answer.

"Hello, Courtney." Sean's voice came on the line.

Everything in her woke up. "I'll buzz you in." She shouldn't be reacting to him this much. She'd only known him a few days while she'd known Lowell for months before getting married and apparently hadn't known him at all.

Then she gobbled down her pie. "Hmm, why did Sean need to be buzzed in when he has the code?" Had she asked that aloud? She gulped some of her mint tea, but it couldn't hide the oops.

"He's being considerate of you," Paisley said quietly, this time without her signature smile.

Ada jumped and shot to the hall, slipping around the corner but staying on her paws.

Unlike the German shepherd, Courtney tried to hold herself back when the doorbell rang. Yet, she'd have run to the door if not for her pesky cast and crutches.

"I can answer the door if you'd like," Paisley offered as she scooped her last bite of pie.

"Yes, please. I don't want to keep him waiting." This time, Courtney didn't ask why he didn't use his house key.

Ada barked joyfully from the hall.

"I hope your day went well." Sean smiled at Courtney as he entered the house holding grocery bags, and her day became a million times better.

Not good. Not good at all. "I shared a cup of tea with Paisley and we ate some of the pie your mother made." She wasn't a great conversationalist, and the sentence sounded mundane. But there had been a time when, with all the scandals and screams, she'd craved mundane. "Can I get you some?" There. That sounded better, didn't it?

Ada jumped at the bags, and Sean lifted them higher. "Sit."

The German shepherd plunked onto her behind, but continued eyeing the bags.

Paisley flashed her signature grin. "Courtney turned out to be a brilliant mechanic."

Heat flamed Courtney's cheeks. "I wouldn't call myself brilliant. Or a mechanic, for that matter."

"Tell that to my truck and those tractors." Then Paisley looked from Sean to Courtney and then back to Sean. "Um, Sean, you might want to put whatever's in those bags in the fridge before something starts melting. And look how time flies. It's time for me to leave."

"Thanks for being here." Sean and Courtney spoke in unison, then glanced at each other.

What was going to melt here was Courtney's heart, and she'd better put it in her self-constructed freezer where it belonged.

Sean opened the door for the quirky programmer. Once she was gone, he locked it, set the alarm again, and gestured to the knotty-pine kitchen where rustic chic met modern convenience. "I'd better follow that advice. You said you weren't picky when I asked what food you liked. So I brought a bit of everything. Well, not everything. Some things." He shifted from one foot to the other, then marched to the kitchen.

Ada dashed after him, slid on the floor again, corrected herself, and trotted slower, her nails clattering against the hardwood.

On her crutches, Courtney followed them. She'd never been fussed over before. It was another unfamiliar—albeit pleasant—feeling. "You didn't have to. Paisley already brought lunch sent by your mother, which was sweet of her. I can put something together for dinner."

"Ada, sit."

Ada sat, but her head moved, following the grocery bags' movement. She probably thought if anything dropped out of bags, it was fair game.

"Um, I hope it's okay that I took the liberty to get takeout." He placed the bags on the marbled counter, then started unloading them.

"That was sweet, actually," she said.

See, she told her inner porcupine. *You can hide your needles.*

She joined him. Then she balked at all the cold cuts, followed by colorful displays of vegetable trays. "You didn't have to buy all this. Maybe take some to your parents' house? Next time, I'll give you a list. Or go with you." She'd have to get a motorized cart. "Though, by the looks of it, the next time won't need to be any time soon."

"You never know. Right now, I live here, too, and I love to eat." He shrugged.

Ada barked as if to say he wasn't the only one, so he gave her a dog treat and washed his hands. The orange aroma from the liquid soap spread through the kitchen, adding to the scent of cucumbers and tomatoes.

"Oh, that's right." Heat rose to her cheeks again. How come she always managed to say the wrong thing? Good thing one didn't have to communicate with a plane verbally.

"I'll go get more groceries from the truck."

"There's more?" She groaned.

Ugh. That sounded ungrateful. Not only was her inner porcupine putting out needles again but also she brought friends along.

Thankfully, he just spread his arms. "Like I said, I love to eat."

Once he was back, she helped put more food away. Including a cake. "That was sweet of you," she said again. "Literally." Maybe she should read some of those novels Genevieve left for her. She clearly needed to learn some new expressions.

"Thanks." His face lit up. Then he took several trips to get everything from the truck. By the time they were done, her stomach was rolling over itself at the wonderful scent of barbecue and onion rings from foam boxes on the breakfast nook table.

"If you don't mind, I'd like to have dinner now." He smiled sheepishly. "I'm starving."

"Me, too."

He said grace, giving her one more reminder of how broken she was. On the contrary, he was so... wholesome. He didn't need to cut himself on the jagged shards she was.

For some time, he talked about the foals they had in August, then about his father's cattle dogs. She listened, then smiled without any effort. Something in her relaxed as she munched on delicious ribs smothered in smoky barbecue, salty french fries awaiting ketchup, and crispy onion rings needing no accompaniment, plus the tangy sweet coleslaw.

She didn't need to talk when she was with him, thinking over every word like she'd had to with Lowell. Sometimes her talk had irritated him. Other times, he hadn't liked her silence because it meant she was upset and what did she have to be upset about when he'd been taking such good care of her? The memory sent a cold shiver over her back, but then Sean's warm gaze made it better.

If she needed to talk to Sean about something, he'd attentively listen. But it was also great to be silent with him. She could simply be. Exist.

"How do you feel about driving around and looking at Christmas lights tonight? And tomorrow, maybe I could leave work at lunchtime, and we can bake Christmas cookies?"

Her lips kicked up at both ideas. And she didn't even like baking. It was difficult to like it after first her father, then her husband, had literally smashed her pies in her face. They'd said her pies weren't that good anyway and they thought smashing pies was funny. It hadn't been. At least, not for her.

"I'm not a good baker," she said as her stomach clenched.

Lowell had said no man would ever like her cooking or baking. That was the reason he'd had to go out so often with friends. Of course, he hadn't bothered to include her in those outings. It was her fault because she was such a drag. Her insides constricted, and she lifted her chin.

"It's not about making perfect cookies. It's about having fun while making them. I, um, already bought the ingredients, including sprinkles. But no biggie if you don't want to. I can give them to Genevieve and Declan or my parents."

Ada barked, which probably meant, "What about me?"

Courtney did her best to brush off her insecurities. Her ex had done a number on her. She picked up another fry. "I'd love to."

"Awesome." Sean grinned at her, sending unexpected butterflies to her tummy. His gaze lingered, adding more butterflies to the mix.

After they cleared the table, he helped her put on her blue parka, and Ada rushed to the door with a leash in her teeth.

"Sorry." Courtney smiled apologetically at the German shepherd. "This is just going to be a car ride."

Ada didn't move, just looked at Courtney with sad eyes.

Courtney rolled her own—both her eyes now opened, so she could roll both. Then she glanced at Sean as she snugged her apple-red hat lower over her ears. "Can we take Ada with us?"

"Sure." He laughed and grabbed the leash. "She has you wrapped around her paw already, doesn't she?" He checked the camera feed on his phone, then opened the front door.

"Yup. And she knows it, too." Courtney embraced the onslaught of cold air.

The baby would've had Courtney wrapped around her pinkie the moment she was born... Grief sliced through Courtney.

Don't think about it. Don't remember. Don't feel.

Barking loudly, Ada dashed outside, and holding the leash, Sean followed at the same speed, though it didn't appear to be entirely voluntary. Courtney's mitten-covered hands gripped her crutches as she hobbled out onto a fresh layer of snow that sparkled in the lanterns' golden glow.

It wasn't good to have to hold onto crutches if she had to fight back. She readjusted her purse with a gun on her shoulder and glanced around, grateful for how well lit the porch was.

Ada ran back to her instead of going into the truck, letting Courtney know she was there and, if anything happened, she'd spot the assailant. Then with Sean, the German shepherd walked nearby, unusually slow for her.

They probably didn't want her to fall. Courtney's eyes watered. After only a few days, she didn't want to lose Sean, though how could one lose someone they never had? And she wanted to keep Ada, but the dog had never been hers, either. Courtney was a temporary guest in their lives, an icy snowflake drifting through that would soon melt away.

Pushing away the yearning, she glanced around again.

If she had to take all these precautions while Sean and Ada were still nearby, what would she have to do when she was on her own again? Her hands in her red-striped mittens clenched tighter on the crutches. Her tongue darted along her split lip, and that was one of the smallest damages.

He didn't offer to carry her from the porch, just like she'd asked him not to, and a significant part of her missed being in his arms. She grunted as she wobbled down the ramp.

She was just frustrated because of the crutches. Right?

"Ada, stay with Courtney." Considerate as always, Sean then brought the truck as close to the ramp as he could, so she had to take only a few steps in the snow.

The German shepherd settled on the backseat floorboards while Courtney rode shotgun.

Once they exited the gate, he glanced her way for a second. "Our parents drove us around the neighborhood every Christmas when we were children."

Her gut twisted at her memories. "Except once, Mom never had the time. And Dad... Maybe it was a good thing he never took us to see Christmas lights, considering how much he drank."

"I'm sorry."

"Not your fault."

"Not your fault either."

Ada barked, so Courtney turned to her. "Not your fault, either."

The German shepherd put her head on her paws as if content it was settled.

Longing stirred in Courtney to lean on someone's shoulder, to feel safe. But she'd given in to that longing before, and look where it had gotten her.

Shivers coursed up her spine, and her stomach knotted. She studied the rearview mirror, then craned her neck to make sure she didn't miss anything. She'd lived like that since she'd left Lowell, and the moment she'd relaxed a bit, the moment she'd started hoping for better, she'd paid a high price. The cost could've been much higher if not for Sean.

"Why do you do all these nice things for me?" She wanted to take in the expression on his face, his eyes, but it was difficult to see in the darkened truck cab. She shifted to the window and stared at the lights forming a reindeer herd in someone's yard.

"No matter how much I wish all these sad things hadn't happened to you, I can't change your past." His voice traveled over the low engine rumble as the truck crept along the brightly lit street. "I can't change your memories. I just hope to help you build happier new ones."

He'd said he wasn't good with words. Yet these words would forever be embroidered in a golden thread on the canvas of her heart just like her name had been embroidered on the Christmas stocking he'd so thoughtfully brought for her.

"That's not a good enough reason," she whispered, more to herself than to him. Now a snowman tried to wave at passersby from another yard, surrounded by oversized snowflakes.

Despite it being a whisper, he must've heard her. "It is to me."

Chapter Seven

In the next yard, multicolored garlands hugged all the trees and shrubs along the front pathway and wrapped around the burgundy window frames and front doorframe. Icicle lights under the roof twinkled and flashed from red and green to golden white.

Ada barked something, but it didn't sound like a warning, more like her stamp of approval for the decorations. Though deep down she might've wondered why no one had put up decorations resembling a German shepherd or any canines.

Something changed in Courtney then as the Christmas lights illuminated a part of her that had remained hidden for so long she hadn't known it existed anymore. No, she hadn't miraculously become open to love again. She hadn't healed. She'd just allowed a bit of hope to ignite. That was a huge step.

Every time things had gotten better during her marriage, reminding her of the sparkling love bubble Lowell had put her in during the beginning of their relationship, it meant they'd get bad again. Every time she'd let her hopes get up, they'd been crushed like that shiny red ornament at her place had been crushed under his ruthless boot.

She took off her mitten and ached to reach for Sean's hand resting on the console while he steered with his other one. But the painfully earned caution kept her from doing it. She peered in the rearview mirror to spot any tail. The rural street remained empty, except for one car that pulled into a yard. She breathed easier, but tension remained.

Would she live all her life like this? But then, if not for Sean, there wouldn't be a life to live. Her hand moved toward his again. For the second time, she stopped herself. She told herself she just needed a little reassurance. But as her heart sped up when he glanced at her for that split second, she knew it was much more. Way much more.

Her heart told her she needed the physical bond with him. But her mind reminded her she couldn't afford it.

"I'm checking the rearview mirror, too. No tail so far," he said.

So he noticed her paranoia.

Frowning, she studied the blazing trail of lights that spelled *Christmas* in the yard ahead. "I used to wince from Lowell's imaginary steps long after I left him. I imagined him at the wheel of every vehicle that stayed behind me a bit longer than I expected."

Ada whined in the back seat as if she understood. She probably didn't, but maybe she felt the anguish in Courtney's tone and wanted to express her support.

Courtney's eyes widened at her own words.

Why did she keep telling him all this? All the things she'd never told anyone. Maybe it was the passerby effect. She could be nothing but a passerby in his life. Just like right now in the car, she was briefly his passenger. Once she healed enough, she'd go back to her life. He'd go back to his. It was easier to share things with someone one knew they'd never see again.

Her rib cage constricted painfully, and not just because of the broken ribs. She wanted to see him again. But why make illusions? If one tried to hold onto shattered rose-tinted glasses, they were guaranteed to cut their fingers.

"Lowell is not here." His voice hardened. "And if he was, we wouldn't let him get to you."

Her heart responded to his protectiveness, and she leaned his way as much as the seat belt allowed. But then, she'd once met a knight in shining armor and had bruises and broken bones to show for it. She bit into her lower lip, then let it go. That lip had suffered enough.

She struggled for a safer topic and a more joyful one. A beautiful sleigh outlined in lights looked magical in the next yard. Well, *all* the lights looked magical.

"I remember Mom driving from the grocery store one Christmas," she said, this time raising her voice. "She took a long route. Maybe it was her way to let us see Christmas lights without upsetting my dad. Me and my sister, Monica, were glued to the windows. A sleigh was one of the lights I saw that night. I asked Mom why we never put any lights in our yard. She said it took too much electricity. But we knew it was because Dad didn't care for Christmas decorations. I could feel by her voice that I upset her. I learned not to ask about the lights. Soon, I also learned not to expect gifts under the tree."

The Christmas lights were as gorgeous as ever, more so because she'd grown up in a poor neighborhood and this one seemed middle-income and had more decorations in the yards. But she didn't have the same awe she'd had as a child, maybe because life's realities had squeezed it out of her little by little until not a single drop remained.

Or maybe the part of her that could feel awe had been gone with Lark. Pain knifed her.

As the truck rumbled forward and more lights filled her vision, she grieved that naïve girl who'd still believed the best in people, open and trusting, who could burst into laughter so easily.

Oh, how much she longed to have even a tiny sparkle of that girl! She grieved the person she used to be and hated the person she became, scared, disillusioned, and lonely. The person who pushed people away because everything in her remembered clawing out for survival and knew another person could always be a threat. A threat she'd needed to protect herself from, if not on a physical level, then on an emotional one. It went triple for tall, broad-shouldered men with strong hands and kind smiles. Because the kind smile could always turn into a cruel one, and the strong hands could become iron fists.

Then she grieved a totally different girl, the feeling much sharper and more painful, something she still couldn't put into words, couldn't completely acknowledge no matter how many years had passed.

She'd never fully made it to the acceptance phase, but when one struggled to survive, precious energy couldn't be spent on analysis of something that could become a tipping point.

Ada whined softly. Worried the German shepherd needed something, Courtney turned to her as much as the seat belt allowed. She was met with sloppy kisses.

"Thanks, darling." Courtney scratched Ada in a sweet spot near her ear and disappeared into her thoughts again. So many things she could've done differently.

Courtney didn't notice how they made it back through the gate and only felt how the truck pulled up to the porch. "Wow, we're back already."

Even if for some time she was lost in her sad thoughts, it mattered to have Sean's silent presence. But the feeling of safety couldn't last, just like the snow outside that would melt by spring or with a warm wind.

He shut off the engine. "I hope you liked the Christmas lights."

"I loved them." Even if the expectations of a miracle didn't return to her. Because what she'd wanted most of all was for the biggest tragedy of her life to reverse, for the loss not to be a loss any longer.

Lowell's words needled her again.

I have something you want.

Could he have meant...?

No, he was baiting her. Reeling her in to come back to him. The part of her that had refused to accept the loss even after years was wishful thinking combined with her inability to cope.

Sean let Ada out, and she shot outside but didn't bark. Hopefully, that meant no intruder lurked nearby. He walked around the vehicle, removed the crutches from the back seat, and opened the door for Courtney. "Sorry. I'm not much of a conversationalist."

"It was perfect." She grasped his hand as he helped her out.

If he'd been cracking jokes in the moments that required silent respect to things so painful she couldn't name them, it would've grated on her nerves. He handed her the crutches.

She was supposed to learn how to navigate walking with crutches better by now, and she did make it okay on the ramp first. Then, somehow, her right crutch slipped with her next step, and she staggered.

Immediately, he was by her, one arm around her waist, supporting her, preventing her from falling. And so was Ada, flanking Courtney from the other side. "Are you okay?"

"Yes." She breathed faster, her warm breath fogging the air in front of her.

Ada barked as if to say she wasn't so sure about that.

His arm tightened around Courtney. "I know you don't want me to carry you inside any longer. But could you at least lean on me for these few steps? Just for my peace of mind?"

Her breathing quickened. "Y–yes. Okay. Sure."

Just "okay" would've sufficed.

Her heart skipped a beat as she leaned on him. The problem wasn't that she didn't want him to carry her. The problem was that she wanted it too much.

He checked the camera footage before entering the house and then let Ada go first. The dog didn't alert to any danger, and part of Courtney relaxed.

Despite her nostalgic mood, she didn't want the evening to end as she entered the lodge that met her with warm air and the aromas of apple pie and pine needles. Or maybe she was just eager to spend a few more minutes in his presence. It could be her present to herself for Christmas, after all.

The best gift ever.

She shook off the mocking thought as he helped her shrug out of her parka. Then she leaned to stroke Ada's fur, and the German shepherd licked her face again, welcoming Courtney home. Tenderness warmed her heart.

Only it wasn't her home.

She breathed in the pine scent. It wasn't her Christmas tree blinking with the lights around ornaments that held so much love and meaning for this family. It wasn't her family, though they had rallied around her.

Leaning on crutches, she straightened out and looked into Sean's mesmerizing eyes. And it wasn't her man.

The thought sliced through her, and she staggered back. And once again, he held her up while Ada flanked her as if not to let her fall.

"Are you okay? Would you like to sit?" Concern etched on his handsome features.

"I'm fine." Courtney spoke sharper than she'd intended.

Hello, porcupine.

She didn't need to be asserting her independence with him.

Ada barked, probably not liking Courtney's tone, either.

She softened her voice as she pulled off her knit hat. "Um, I believe we still have lots of your mother's apple pie left. Would you like to share it?"

Surprise flashed in his brown eyes, followed by a grin, while he took off her one boot. "I'd love to."

He might've been surprised because she'd never suggested they do anything together before.

"Let me help you with your scarf." He straightened to his full height, towering over her. That used to scare her on a subconscious level, but now more and more, she felt protected instead. It would be so easy to lose her guard.

As he unraveled her scarf, his fingers touched her neck by accident, and in turn, that unraveled a pleasant feeling inside her.

What was happening? For a long time, she'd been terrified of a man's touch, and here she longed for it. Steeling herself against the feeling, she moved away, then turned around.

"Sure." He unwound his scarf and shrugged out of his coat, but his focus stayed on her.

"Let's get cocoa and pie."

"Sure," he said again, then followed her into the kitchen, though she walked excruciatingly slow.

Ada stretched nearby, then joined them, as well.

He was straightforward and didn't expect any underhanded tactics from her. She'd been so used to Lowell's words having a double meaning and his games having rules only he knew. Now, Sean's openness and sincerity were as refreshing as the first snowfall. She no longer had to think over her every word, knowing whatever she'd said could still be twisted to imply things she'd never meant.

For years, she hadn't just walked on eggshells. She'd walked on the edges of a thousand knives. Yet she'd now crawl on the edges of a thousand knives if she could only bring back that fateful night she'd lost her baby.

She swallowed around the lump in her throat. At least, she could think about it now without feeling like she'd collapse.

She placed pie slices on plates while he made cocoa. She watched his hands as they poured the cocoa mix into hot water, such mundane movements, but meaningful to her because before she'd had difficulty looking at men's hands. Everything in her used to recoil because a subconscious part of her was ready for those hands to become fists and hit her.

Yet when she looked at his hands, she imagined them petting Ada, nudging his brother's shoulder, or helping her with her crutches and parka. She could easily imagine them taking care of foals and calves with tenderness. And she remembered them holding her while he carried her. She still felt that fleeting touch of his fingertips on her neck and was desperate to feel it again. A flutter appeared in her belly.

With Sean, she could see how something other men used for destruction could be used for joy.

She glanced at the cup, not sure she could get the cocoa to the destination without spilling hot liquid on herself. "Could we eat the pie near the Christmas tree, please? I know it might sound ridiculous."

In the beginning, Lowell had been so supportive. But after they'd married, he'd often made fun of her requests. Anything she'd asked for was ridiculous. Or silly.

"Of course. As you say, why not? I'll put everything on a tray and bring it." True to his word, he balanced the cups with steaming cocoa and the plates with pie and forks on a tray.

Then he walked to the living room and set the tray on the carpet. Courtney almost feared Ada would rush to the sweet pie and stomp on it or slurp at it. But the noble German shepherd just trotted into the living room, then stretched on the carpet, and stayed in a regal pose a decent distance from the tree and the tray.

"Good girl," Courtney whispered in her direction, then wobbled to Sean with way less speed and grace than Ada. Getting down onto the carpet in front of the Christmas tree proved more difficult as an adult with a cast than as an agile child with limber legs. But with Sean's help, she managed.

She scooped a bite of the apple pie, enjoying the sweet gooeyness. "One year, when I was little and things weren't too horrible, Mom let me and Monica eat a pie under the tree on Christmas Eve. We even got seconds. We told each other stories and wondered what presents we were going to get. We fell asleep under the tree, and Dad later carried us to bed one by one. It was a wonderful day."

He drank some of his cocoa. "I hope all your days in your life from now on will be wonderful."

"It's impossible," she whispered. She picked up her cup and tested a few careful sips.

"I'm blessed. Every day is wonderful to me. Of course, there are stressful days. And some are difficult or sad. But there's something wonderful in every day." He paused. Then his voice dipped. "My days with you are more wonderful than others."

Her heart stuttered. She practically dropped her fork. She hid her feelings behind the cocoa cup and gulped sips of hot liquid. "Thank you." She pushed her half-eaten pie aside and moved closer to him along the carpet. "My days are much better now. Thanks to you."

Emotion darkened his brown eyes. The desire to kiss him became almost irresistible, shocking her. After her divorce, it'd been a huge challenge even to stay in a man's presence without the urge to run.

On the contrary, Sean had a pull on her she couldn't explain. Or maybe she could. He was kind to her. That was all. So little and yet so much.

If only there was mistletoe dangling over them. Then she'd have an excuse to lean into his touch, into his kiss. Her every cell was drawn to him beyond measure. She licked her lips, and her pulse skyrocketed when his eyes widened and he tucked a strand of hair behind her ear.

It took all her willpower and then some to pull away. She slid back on the carpet as disappointment ripped through her. Disappointment with the kiss that never happened. Disappointment with herself that she'd let it go this far.

"We... shouldn't... I... Well, you know." She fidgeted with strands on the soft rug. "And my lip still hasn't healed completely and all."

If he wasn't a good conversationalist, then she was a disastrous one.

Hurt flashed in his eyes, but he nodded. "I understand. I'd never push you into anything you're not ready for. I hope you know that."

"Yes." She was the one who wanted to leap into his protective, tender arms and stay there. But she couldn't. And she shouldn't want to. She'd promised herself she'd stand on her own two feet, and she needed to keep that promise.

Later, after he'd put everything away and she'd fed Ada, Courtney reluctantly retired to her room. While she'd let her regular clients know she wouldn't be accepting bookings for flights and had canceled the ones already booked, she needed to check her work email for any requests. Especially considering she'd had to leave her phone behind and get a burner so Lowell wouldn't be able to track her cell phone. Since clients wouldn't be able to reach her by phone or text, only via email, her business would take a hit.

After getting her laptop, she made herself comfortable on her bed while Ada kept her company on the nearby rug, nearly blending in with the wolves howling on its print. Courtney answered several emails before a new one pinged her inbox. She gasped at the subject line.

I have something you want.

With trembling fingers, she opened it, and her stomach dropped. There was only one sentence there and a photo.

The sentence read: *Or is it somebody?* The photo was of baby feet. It could easily be a stock photo downloaded online, and yet Courtney felt like she stopped breathing.

Chapter Eight

Sean couldn't figure out why Courtney looked so gloomy the next day. While they had lunch in silence, her mouth was pressed in a thin line, and her shoulders slumped forward. Her chocolate-brown hair fell on her face, and she didn't push it back as if she wanted to hide behind its curtain. She seemed to be lost in her own world, and when he tried to liven the situation by asking questions, he'd had to ask twice before she reacted.

She did smile at Ada when she'd helped wash the dog after he'd taken Ada for a walk. But even that smile was sad.

His heart sank to the tile as he lined up cookie ingredients on the marbled-gray counter, unsure whether it was worth it to start this project. He'd planned a fun day for them. So far, it had seemed anything but that.

His hand opening the knotty-pine cabinet stilled. Was it because of their near kiss? Or was she upset about something else? He brought out the flour canister and the egg carton.

But then, who was he to commandeer her mood? And it wasn't like she didn't have a long list of things to be upset about. He just hated seeing her sad.

At some point, he'd have to see her gone. The mere thought stabbed him, and he almost dropped the eggs.

Should he leave her alone or ask her if he could help? This was new territory to him. With his friends and family, they'd always been direct.

He walked from the kitchen to the living room and found her slouched over her laptop on the sofa. Unlike in the morning, her chocolate-brown hair was pinned by her nape now. That underscored the delicate outline of her face and made her large blue eyes stand out even more. Her black turtleneck and black slacks might've been what caused her to look paler than usual. He didn't want to think of any other reason.

Ada stretched on the carpet near Courtney's feet, protective as always. Clearly, the German shepherd had adopted Courtney into the family, and that made Sean smile. Then Courtney looked up, and the full power of the hurt in her blue eyes slammed into him and slapped the smile from his face.

He'd ask whether he could help and then leave her alone. He leaned to the German shepherd, who was in her usual noble posture, and stroked her short fur, then looked up at Courtney. "Anything I can help you with?"

This time, he didn't have to ask the question twice.

Slowly, as if every movement took an effort, she shifted back and lifted her gaze from the laptop screen. Her thoughts still seemed to be somewhere else. "I—You wanted to bake cookies today, didn't you?"

He had a feeling cookies were way low on her priority list right now. "We don't have to. I mean, if you're busy. Or don't feel like it. Or not interested. I mean…" He cringed. He needed to improve his speaking skills. Good thing he wasn't a teacher like Genevieve, or it would have taken many lessons before the students understood what he meant. Or he'd be wasting time on explaining the same things in three different ways, like today.

"I get the idea." The corners of her lips fluttered up. "You know what?" Then she said the phrase that seemed to be her favorite. "Why not?"

His spirit lifted a little. "Why not, indeed?"

He handed her the crutches, and they walked to the kitchen. Ada stayed in the living room, which Sean appreciated because it wasn't a good idea for a dog to be near the food preparation.

He got the mixer from the shelf.

"If you don't mind, I'd rather do it by hand. I'm used to doing it this way." She started beating two eggs with a whisk, balancing on one leg.

He suppressed a grimace. He should've considered her broken leg before suggesting this activity. He just wanted to spend more time with her and share a family tradition. "Let me bring you a chair you can brace your knee on as you stand. Or I can take all the ingredients to the breakfast nook where you can sit, and we can work there."

"The chair would be great."

He rushed to the dining room. Strangely enough, even after only a few days, she already felt like part of the family. He could imagine them cooking breakfast together, then sharing it in his breakfast nook overlooking the lawn with wildflowers in summer. He could smell the bacon already, taste the orange juice. It was such a simple dream, maybe mundane to others, but his heart yearned for it.

His dreams were simple. He'd never dreamed of seeing the world like Declan or protecting it like Cormac. Sean was content with being a cowboy, working on the land where he'd grown up, and feeding the country. He still wanted all that. Only since he'd met Courtney, she'd become the central part of his dream—the central and impossible part. And that made the yearning all the stronger.

He placed the chair in front of her and eyed the products. "I'll get sugar." He picked it up from the shelf.

"I received an email from my ex-husband yesterday. On my work email address." Courtney's words made him spin around.

He plopped down the sugar canister. No wonder she looked rattled. Hadn't the guy done enough damage? Why couldn't he leave her alone? The only bright side in this was that, if they managed to track Lowell, maybe they could make him answer for his crimes.

With raw heat surging through him, Sean nearly growled like Ada. "What did he want?"

Her eyes widened, and she stumbled back against the counter. Then her arms flew in front of her to protect herself. Her pupils dilated, and she took a deep breath as if to calm herself. She gripped the gray marble with such force her knuckles went white. Then she sank onto the chair.

Oh man! He groaned. "I didn't mean to scare you. I'm sorry."

He ached to take her into his arms, to comfort her, and his heart skipped a beat at the thought. He shouldn't, of course. And now his embrace probably wouldn't be welcome because, on a subconscious level, she'd see him as a threat.

"It's... it's okay." Her split lower lip trembled. "I know you didn't mean to. It's just when a man raises his voice, I... Well, you know."

"I know. I–I just don't want you to get hurt." He had less finesse than a proverbial bull in a china shop. He did his best to rephrase his question in a much calmer tone. "Is it okay to ask what he wrote?" Heat crept up his neck. "I mean, unless it's too personal. Or something you don't want to share. Or I don't know...." Make that a whole bunch of bulls in a *tiny* china shop.

"I get the idea." Her expression unreadable, she stood and braced her knee on the chair's seat, so she could reach the counter. Then she measured a cup and a half of sugar and added an equal amount of butter. Once she'd creamed that, she poured in the eggs.

"It was... Well, there's a lot of backstory to try to explain what he meant. Or maybe it's my imagination. Or my guilty conscience." She sprinkled in the teaspoons of salt, baking powder, and vanilla and beat the batter smooth again. Sweet vanilla scented the air.

Why would she possibly have a guilty conscience? He spread wax paper across the marbled counter to roll the batter on. "I'm here if you're comfortable sharing it. We can go sit in the living room instead. Forget about the cookies. Or *I* can finish making them."

"It's okay. You should preheat the oven, though. I–I want to be doing something. I never told anyone about this story before. Well, I didn't really have anyone to share it with." She swallowed hard, then folded in three cups of flour. "Okay, the email subject line said, 'I have something you want.' He said the same thing when he beat me up the other day. Then I didn't pay much attention for the obvious reason, being distracted by the pain he inflicted."

Fierce heat surged through Sean again, but he subdued it and turned his back to set the oven, so she couldn't see anything his expression revealed in case he didn't subdue it enough. Yet a few unkind words about Lowell slipped in a mutter.

Ada growled from the living room as if she'd heard him.

Then he remembered he was supposed to be helping here and placed packages of multicolored and red and green sprinkles on the counter and brought out a rolling pin and box of cookie cutters.

She scooped cookie dough onto the wax paper. "Then in the body of the email, he wrote, 'Or *someone* you want.'"

"Does he still think you'd go to him after all he's done?" The words slipped out before he could stop them. But then, hadn't many women stayed with the abuser? Even gone back to them.

At some point, he could accept that he'd lose her, that she'd leave and literally fly away. But when it happened, he could hope she'd become happy eventually, even if it wasn't with him. He couldn't bear the thought of losing her to harm.

"He didn't mean *that*." Her hand stopped moving, then resumed rolling dough. "At least, I don't think he did. Five years ago, I lost a baby. I miscarried." She tilted her head, her gaze dewy behind damp lashes, then straightened her shoulders as if she needed to be on his eye level. "Her name was Lark, my little songbird."

So much pain was in her eyes.

His jaw slackened, and he couldn't stop himself. He gathered her in his arms and held her close. "I'm so sorry for your loss. I'm so sorry." The words seemed insignificant compared to what she'd experienced. The festive sprinkles mocked the tragedy.

Was her clothing choice today because she was mourning anew?

She didn't pull away but leaned into him. He stroked her back, wishing he could somehow lessen her pain. For several minutes, he cradled her, praying over her.

Then she eased out of his embrace and leaned against the counter. "I know what you think. How come I didn't leave him to protect the baby inside me while knowing he was abusive?"

"I didn't think that at all." He grasped her hand and held it, hoping he could somehow transfer some of his strength to her.

She left her hand in his for a few moments, then slid free, and regret jolted through him. Her hand trembling, she started cutting the cookies with a Christmas-tree-shaped cutter.

"May I?" He raised an angel-shaped cutter.

"Sure." She checked on the oven. "Looking back, I should've left. The baby wasn't planned but was such a joy to me nonetheless. It didn't matter that I didn't have anywhere to go. Or that he controlled all our finances. Or that I was isolated from friends and family."

"That was so wrong." Lavalike heat sluiced through his veins. But again, he managed to keep it under the surface. Well, except that he cut some of the dough with such force he mangled the innocent angel cookies. Like her husband had mangled the innocent angels in his care.

Sean gentled his touch since no man should ever hurt an angel, even a cookie-dough one.

Her hand trembling less now, she sprinkled red and green on the Christmas-tree cookies. "I decided that, if he hit me from then on, I'd leave. I'd go to the women's shelter and figure out the way. But the news changed him, made him softer again. Not like in the time of dating, but much better than it had become. And silly me, I thought he'd change for the baby. It was going to be his child, after all. And for some time, it was that way."

Matching her, he salted the angels with multicolored sprinkles and edged their wings back into proper shape before transferring them to the tray. He rattled the tray into the oven and set the timer without saying a word.

She gestured to the living room. "Would you mind if we sit on the sofa now?"

"Sure. I mean, of course, I don't mind." He followed her to the living room.

She lowered herself onto the sofa and braced the crutches nearby, then hugged a pink throw pillow. The Christmas-tree lights and crackling fire bathed her in an angelic glow. "Without noticing it, I fell into the familiar pattern of doing my best to placate him. To keep him happy. He did a good job reminding me the baby needed the good life only he could give it. He was a good provider, after all.

"So, while at first I balked at his idea of me giving birth at home, I relented. He knew a woman named Naomi Bricker whom he said was an excellent midwife. He introduced us, and she seemed courteous and friendly. I could do it in the comfort of my own home. He went to all my gynecological appointments. Held my hand during the sonogram. Went ecstatic when we discovered we were expecting a girl. I'd worried because I suspected he wanted a son. Eventually, giving birth at home seemed to be an argument I couldn't win. I reluctantly agreed."

Knowing what was coming made the news gut-wrenching. His heart went out to her, and he reached for her hand. This time, she didn't remove it, and it felt like a milestone. As desperately as he searched for the right words to comfort her, he didn't find any, so he had to settle for compassionate silence. She didn't seem to expect anything else.

She looked straight ahead at the crackling fire, but based on her absent gaze, she'd been looking into the past. "We still argued sometimes when I asked him to do more around the house because I couldn't, but he said it was part of every marriage. And I didn't know any better. I only knew it was a huge improvement over what it was before, so I persuaded myself I should be grateful.

"When I went into labor, I changed my mind and begged him to take me to the hospital. He said I'd be fine and he'd called the midwife and she'd be there right away. She'd worked at the hospital and delivered plenty of babies. She had the license. Our daughter and I would be fine. Naomi showed up fast, indeed. I had a weird premonition, but I told myself I had no choice at that point. Labor had taken many hours, and I did my best to push. Then she said she'd inject me with medicine to help me relax and help with the pain. I tried to protest, but she assured me it wouldn't harm the baby. Lowell said it would be fine and not to worry."

His voice sharpened. "What did she inject you with?"

A sheen glowed in her eyes, and she blinked fast fighting back tears. "I don't know. I pushed again and again. Then it's blurry. It was like floating in a dream. Finally, I gave birth. But... my precious little girl didn't cry. I begged them to give her to me. But Naomi took the baby away. When she came back, she said she was sorry and the baby was stillborn."

He squeezed her hand, wishing with all his heart he could help her.

"I started screaming and thrashing, and Lowell held me down while Naomi injected something to calm me down. I don't remember much of what happened for two weeks afterward. I couldn't face reality. In some kind of mental fog, I either slept or cried. I didn't want to believe what happened. He gave me pills saying they'd help me feel better."

Sean grunted. "He drugged you."

Tears spilled from her eyes and floated over her cheeks, catching the Christmas-tree lights and breaking his heart. "I shouldn't have taken them, but I didn't have the strength to refuse. I needed oblivion, even if I didn't deserve it. I kept imagining that, if I hadn't agreed to his suggestion of delivering the baby at home, Lark might've lived—might've laughed and played, and sang."

"It wasn't your fault." He reached for the tissue box from the coffee table as suspicions roiled him. Several things about that delivery sounded fishy.

The timer pinged on the stove, and she waved him away to rescue the cookies.

When he returned, she was pressing the tissue to her eyes, and he handed her another one as fresh tears spilled over. "It's difficult to stop self-blame. When I started thinking straight again, I asked for Lark to be buried, and he said I'd already agreed to her cremation. Then weeks later, things started getting horrible again. I couldn't just bounce back and recover, and he got furious that a hot dinner didn't wait for him as usual after his hard work. That I didn't clean the house. When I told him I needed to recover, he yelled at me, at how useless I was.

"I forced myself to move and do things for him. If I tried to talk about the baby, it irritated him. So I stopped. And even thinking about Lark was painful, anyway. But I couldn't do as much as I did before giving birth. So the shouting started again. We were going back to normal, to what apparently was normal for our marriage. He started hitting the wall again. Then... then it wasn't the wall."

"I'm so sorry." He shifted closer, desperate to take away her pain but having no clue how.

She picked up another tissue as she sobbed. "It was getting worse. I found myself wishing to get pregnant again, not just because of the baby but also because of that lull when I wasn't getting hit. Then I realized how horrible that sounded. And that once born, my baby wouldn't be safe with him. It had taken Dad years to start hitting us, but it happened nonetheless. I managed to squirrel some funds away during the next several months. Then I left for the women's shelter. It still took me a long time to go to sleep without crying."

She tucked her face against his shirt and kept sobbing. He wrapped his arms around her, everything in him desperate to help her and equally desperate to know how. Probably telling her he suspected her baby didn't die that day wouldn't help.

She pushed back and looked up at him, tears glistening on her face. "I had a weird feeling about the day of delivery. But thinking about the loss was so painful that I pushed it away. Lowell's email brought it back. If... if it was him, of course. What if Lowell didn't want the baby like he said he did? Before we married, he said he wanted children. But after we got married, he made me get on birth control. I thought when I got pregnant accidentally, he changed his mind again and was happy with it. But... what if he didn't?"

Sean draped his arm across her shoulders. "Do you know how to find the midwife?"

"Naomi gave me her phone number. When I called her two months after the birth, the number was disconnected. When I asked Lowell about it, he said she must've changed her phone. And why would I need to talk to her anyway?"

"What about calling the hospital where she worked?"

"I didn't call them at the time. I looked at their website today and called them. They told me they couldn't divulge information about their staff. Which is understandable." She looked away. "Am I imagining things? Thinking my daughter..."

When she didn't finish the sentence, he did it for her. "Might still be alive."

Chapter Nine

Courtney couldn't believe her ears. "What?"

Though why was she so surprised? Deep down, she'd suspected what Paisley just confirmed.

Sean moved closer as if to protect her from another blow.

The quirky computer programmer with pink-and-blue hair blinked at Courtney apologetically, then readjusted her butterfly headband. Not surprisingly, pink butterfly decals floated over her blue sweater as if frolicking in an azure sky. "I'm sorry. A person with the name Naomi Bricker never worked at that hospital."

Courtney didn't ask how Paisley knew. Apparently, she could get into private information databases. She assured Courtney that she'd only done it once in years and only for the dire need of someone's well-being.

Her knees wobbly, Courtney sank onto the sofa. Her crutches slipped from her hands and thudded on the hardwood flooring. Sean picked them up and positioned them near her. Ada walked over and nuzzled her head on Courtney's lap in a sweet show of support.

Her mind whirling, she petted the dog. "I can't believe my stupidity. I should've asked for her ID. I should've insisted on seeing her midwife license."

Sean sat near her and clasped her hand while Ada stretched at their feet. "You're not stupid. Lots of people fall victim to their abusers' manipulations—not because of stupidity but because of believing in people and trusting them."

Courtney barely resisted the temptation to lean into him. The mere connection of his simple touch did strange things to her heart while her emotions were raw.

"That's true." Paisley's hazel gaze softened as she placed a protective hand over her belly. "I've seen it firsthand in the project I've been working on. So no need for self-blame. There's also the probability that she'd have shown a fake one. It's not too difficult to get a fake ID if you know the right people to ask and are willing to pay the needed price."

Again, Courtney didn't ask how Paisley knew that.

"I need to find Naomi Bricker. Or... whatever her real name is." Easier said than done. Courtney knew nothing about the woman, not even her name. The woman's experience delivering babies might've been a lie, as well.

Pain sliced through her. What happened to her baby? Was it wrong to allow even a sliver of hope that Lark was still alive?

Was it false hope, based on another web of Lowell's lies? On this emotional roller coaster, Courtney felt like the safety belts were missing and she was about to fall out and hit the ground from a dangerous height. Then Sean squeezed her hand, and the gesture grounded her, stopped the room from spinning.

He was her much-needed rock in this time adrift. But then, hadn't she considered Lowell her rock once, as well?

The best gift ever.

Her gut twisted.

Sean's eyes lit up. "One of my brothers, Brandon, is a self-taught artist. Maybe he can draw Naomi's portrait."

Courtney nearly jumped to her feet, then remembered the crutches. "Can we do it now?"

Then she deflated. "I do appreciate the offer, but what good will a sketch do if we have nobody to show it to?"

Sean rubbed his forehead. "Well, Naomi might've worked at that hospital's neonatal department as a nurse, just under a different name. Was your impression that she had the skills needed for delivering babies?"

"I think so." Courtney nodded slowly. Her head seemed to weigh a ton, and every movement still felt like it took an enormous effort. "And I don't think Lowell would risk getting someone with zero knowledge of childbirth." Or was that another sample of her naïve thinking?

Could Lark be alive? Courtney's world tilted on its axis, and she didn't know what to think.

"Here we go." Paisley made a cutting gesture with her hand. "Or she might've worked at a different hospital. Or not. Once I have a sketch to work with, I'll run it against facial recognition software for images on the internet. We'll figure it out."

Hope unraveled inside Courtney, pushing out slowly and painstakingly like a butterfly from its cocoon, and she was still afraid to believe its quiet whisper. "Thank you so much."

He fished out his phone and typed something. Seconds later, an incoming text chimed. He read it, nodded to himself, and tucked his phone away. "Brandon was working at the ranch, but he'll be here in a few minutes with his art supplies."

Her jaw slackened. "Just like that? Your brother will drop everything and rush here to help me?"

"Of course." He shrugged like it was nothing special. "I told him it was urgent."

She gaped. Nothing special? It was *very* special to her. Even in the best of times when she hadn't ruined her relationship with her sister, they'd never been like that. She wasn't used to people dropping everything else and doing things for her. It was usually the other way around.

But she didn't have the time to ponder it or long for family ties like his because finding Lark was her priority. Her rib cage constricted painfully, and not because of the broken ribs. Or was she kidding herself by imagining her daughter was still alive? Was it an illusion because Courtney couldn't handle her grief?

"My cop brother is on his shift now," Sean said. "He can help by asking around using his connections. His wife is a police officer, as well. I'm sure she wouldn't mind helping. Are you sure you don't want to make an official report?"

She winced, knowing better, but shook her head. "No."

"You're not sure?" He shifted closer, giving her a whiff of the simple and intoxicating scent of hay and leather.

She longed to hide in the safe circle of his arms, still against his chest, and just the thought increased her yearning. He represented the safety and protection she'd sought since being a scared little girl and had never found. But she couldn't allow herself to do it.

Her abusive marriage should've been her lesson that the only person she could rely on was herself.

She shook her head again. No wonder Lowell always said she was horrible at communication. She'd had difficulty getting her point across, but it might've been because people rarely listened to her while she'd been growing up. She'd been a nuisance to her older sister who'd gotten stuck babysitting her often, and

Courtney had been just another mouth to feed to her father. On the plus side, he'd taught her what kind of parent she didn't want to be.

Only, for a long time, she'd been persuaded she hadn't managed to save the precious life inside her.

Was she making another mistake by not going to the police now? "I meant, I don't want to make an official report because I don't want to spook Lowell. If Lark is alive and with him, he might relocate somewhere I'd never find."

His jaw set tight. Clearly, he didn't approve of her decision.

She'd better further explain. "Maybe it's just deep-rooted memories of my father screaming at my mother." A shudder went through her. "The police apprehended my father on several occasions after he beat up Mom. The first few times, the neighbors called the police. Mom never called the police herself because he promised he'd beat her to a pulp if she did.

"Then one time, um, *I* called the police. Mom refused to file against him every time. Said she fell. She always said that. The officers apprehended him but had to let him go. He came home and made me watch him hit her. A lot." She flinched. "And every time he hit her that night, he said it was my fault. Later, as I held towel-wrapped packs of frozen peas to her bruises, I cried and begged her forgiveness. She said we had to survive on our own. That she just needed to find a way not to make him angry."

His dark eyes glossed. "I'm so sorry that happened to you. You know it wasn't your fault, right?"

"Yes, I know it," her voice dipped. "But I don't *feel* it."

Paisley's hazel eyes dimmed, as well. "It's horrible. But it's a different situation now."

Courtney struggled for a compromise. What would be the best decision for her daughter? "I'll go to the police once we have more information. There's not much for them to investigate right now." Then her mind latched onto something else. She turned toward Paisley so abruptly she nearly knocked down her crutches again. "You're some kind of computer genius, right?"

"Maybe." Paisley's posture stiffened as if she knew what was coming.

Courtney's mind raced. "Would you be able to track down where the emails Lowell supposedly sent me came from? The IP address location or something?"

Paisley exchanged glances with Sean. Courtney's stomach dipped. They could be protective of her—well, Sean *was* protective of her for sure. They might not want her to know Lowell's location because she'd go to him if it meant finding out whether her baby was still alive. Courtney's heart squeezed in her chest.

Well, Lark wouldn't be a baby any longer. Her songbird would be almost four years old. If she was alive, who'd been taking care of her? Was it good care, or was she crying right now somewhere in the world, wishing she had her mommy? Everything in Courtney shattered. If only she were like a bird who could just fly to her little one.

Meanwhile, Sean raised an eyebrow. "Emails as in plural? There were several?"

She looked away, then forced herself to meet his gaze as a heavier weight pressed on her chest, making it more difficult to breathe. "Yes. I answered him. I emailed, 'Who is this? What do you mean?'"

"It's not a good idea to engage with Lowell. Or with some scammer." Sean exchanged glances with Paisley again, and deeper lines etched into his handsome features.

Paisley's voice softened. "Besides, you know he might be able to track down *your* IP address, as well, right?"

That might lead him to this small town. Great. Was her entire life one long series of mistakes?

"I'm sorry." Courtney hugged herself and resisted the urge to hang her head. Answering Lowell—if that was even him—wasn't her brightest idea by far. And the last thing she wanted was to bring danger to Sean's doorstep or his family. They'd been nothing but kind to her, and *this* was the way she'd repaid them?

No matter what she did, someone had gotten hurt. Her mother. Her sister—like when Lowell had gotten Monica fired because she'd interfered in Courtney's marriage. Courtney's precious little girl. And now it could be Sean's family.

"I felt I needed to do something at least. If there's even a sliver of a chance of finding Lark, please, please help me. Even if I don't deserve it," she added in a lower voice. Rebuilding her confidence took a huge effort, and now, it was slipping away.

"You deserve everything. You deserve the world." Sean clasped her hand in silent support and squeezed her fingers. "And you know we'll do everything to help you. We just don't want anything to happen to you."

His words and gestures sent a much-needed wave of reassurance through her. But was she pushing him too far? Was she taking advantage of his attraction to her? So badly, she wanted to lean into him, to step into his embrace. But if she did, she'd become a weeping mess. With an effort, she held her head high.

Then he asked, "What was his reply?"

She frowned, more weight pressing on her sternum because what she'd received wasn't worth the risk. "Just three words—'Care to guess?'"

"Um, I don't know how to guess those words." Sean's fingers stroked her hand.

Yup. Ada had better communication skills than Courtney did. She cleared her throat. "That was his reply. 'Care to guess?'"

Paisley squirmed in her seat. "Okay, I'll look at it. Some people know how to cover their tracks, though."

"But you know how to, what, uncover them, right?" Courtney turned a pleading gaze at Paisley. "Please? I won't use that information if we can find Naomi first. This would be the last resort."

Paisley didn't look convinced.

So Courtney continued, letting desperation slip into her voice. "Please. I need to know. I won't even be able to breathe normally until I know. I've been separated from Lowell for three years, divorced for two and a half. Did he get her back after I left him? Or did he leave her with whoever was raising her while I was still with him? What if they treated her badly? Or if he got her back and abused her like he did me? She's an innocent child."

A muscle moved in Sean's cheek. "If we find him, I'm going with you. You're not going to be in this alone."

She managed to hold in tears before, but now they sprang to her eyes. She was getting too weepy, and she didn't need to open the floodgates like she'd done yesterday. She did her best to hold them in.

He wiped the tear that did escape, his touch gentle on her skin, but it still traveled to her very core. His words meant the world to her. Yet deep down, she knew she couldn't allow him to go with her. He'd become too dear to her already. She'd never want to see him hurt, even though she'd be the one hurting him if she left. But she couldn't put his life at risk.

As the man of integrity he was, he'd want to shield her. Her feelings for him grew, but it wasn't about her right now but about her little girl.

A chill gripped her heart. She'd give up her life for Lark, but would it be enough?

There was something else. Without noticing, she reached the point where she needed Sean much more than he needed her, even if she'd done her best not to show it. Lowell had told her many times how needy she was when all she'd wanted was to love him. She couldn't fall into that trap again. Couldn't have that imbalance of power.

"Okay. I'll need your laptop." Paisley sighed, but it sounded like resignation, not irritation. "No guarantees, though. And from now on, before you reply to any suspicious message, let me first cover your tracks. Also, I don't want to give you false hope. It might just be someone sending spam and not Lowell at all."

Even minuscule hope was better than no hope at all.

"Thank you so much!" Courtney rushed to her bedroom to pick the laptop up, or at least rushed as much as she could on crutches.

By the time she hobbled back with her laptop under her armpit, Brandon was there.

She set her laptop down, balanced on one leg and one crutch, and shook his hand. "Thank you for agreeing to help me. And for coming here so fast."

"I'm glad to be able to help." He settled in the armchair with a large sheet of paper and pencils.

She logged on to the laptop for Paisley, though she wasn't sure the quirky computer programmer needed her login credentials. Then her gaze landed on Sean, who leaned against the fireplace now, and their gazes met and held. The depth of worry and compassion in those malty-brown depths tugged at her. She drew a deep breath of air filled with his scent, her pulse quickening. But once again, she couldn't afford a distraction. Her head pounded with the urgency to find Lark.

She averted her gaze to Brandon. "How does this work? I need to describe parts of the face, right? The hairstyle?"

"I'm not a professional sketch artist. But yes, that's basically how it works."

Paisley tapped her fingernails on the keyboard. The azure-hued butterflies appeared to dance on the nail polish with her spritely movement. "There's a new reply. 'Does the name Lark tell you anything? Or would you like a photo?'"

The world stopped moving in front of Courtney's eyes.

Paisley's voice hardened. "I'm guessing you want me to reply with a yes."

Chapter Ten

Courtney tossed and turned the entire night, disappearing into a fitful slumber from time to time, then waking up to check her phone for emails from Lowell. There were other emails, but none from that address. When she did manage to sleep, she dreamed of a little girl with chocolate-brown pigtails screaming for her mommy, a little girl lost and scared. A thousand thoughts roiled in Courtney's mind like angry wasps, disturbed from their nest and ready to sting, some stinging already.

What if Lowell had only been teasing her, trying to lure her back in? What if her hopes would be crushed? How could she survive losing her daughter a second time?

But if there was even a minuscule chance—the size of the wasp's stinger—that her daughter was alive and might need Courtney's help, Courtney would crawl to the other side of the earth for her.

By early morning, her head was pounding, and she slipped out of the bed with its sunshine-yellow bedsheets. It was anything but sunshine in her soul. Could this still lead to sunrise not just of a new day but of a new life with Sean? She couldn't even hope for that while all her attention had to concentrate on her daughter possibly being alive.

She switched on the light, and her distorted reflection stared at her from a gold-tinted ornament on the pine branch. The pine aroma was supposed to be calming, but now a whole forest of pine trees wouldn't calm her. Especially after she'd seen Lark running through such a forest in the darkness, terrified.

It was still dark outside, but according to Courtney's watch, it was six in the morning. She couldn't stay in bed any longer. Her entire body was pulsing with the urgency to find her daughter, to ensure she was all right.

That was, if her hopes weren't another illusion she'd told herself, like Lowell's love. As fleeting as her dreams.

Tears burned behind her eyes, but she held them in as she drew her crutches carefully. She didn't want to drop them and wake Sean. Even though yearning filled her heart at the mere thought of him.

She couldn't permit that yearning to claim her. She brushed her teeth furiously in the bathroom, the toothpaste's refreshing mint flavor not enough to distract her. Searching for Lark had to consume her.

Then she splashed some cold water on her face. She needed a clear mind today more than ever, but just cold water couldn't help. Maybe a pond of coffee would.

After a million overnight thoughts, she had a new reason to tamp down her growing attraction to Sean, no matter how supportive he was, or how desperate she was to lean on his broad shoulders. Or, let's face it, how drawn she was to him. Her pulse quickened as if anticipating seeing him in a few minutes.

If they couldn't find Naomi Bricker but found Lowell's location, Courtney would have to go to him alone. She could risk her own life, not Sean's. She'd have to leave without letting him know.

She shuddered at the mere idea of seeing her ex-husband again, nearly letting the brush slip out of her hand. Her subconscious remembered the beatings, insults, and humiliation, even if her mind tried to forget. Fear settled in her bones, including the broken ones. Especially the broken ones.

She scowled at her reflection with dark circles under her eyes and a busted lip as she brushed her hair with more force than necessary, ripping out a few extra hairs. Her scowl deepened. If Lowell wasn't here to punish her, did she have to keep punishing herself?

Her gaze dropped to her makeup on the sink counter.

First, she'd learned how to apply makeup to be pretty for Lowell. Then it had been a necessity to hide bruises. Her hand moved toward a tube of pink lipstick. Her lip was healing somewhat, and a large part of her was eager to look pretty for Sean.

No.

As much as she wanted him to like her, or... more, it was a bad idea. And a cruel one. Making him like her wasn't fair to him. Because most likely she'd have to rip apart one more bond she'd been forming. She'd had to abandon any person she'd loved. Apparently, it was her life.

But not Lark. She couldn't abandon her songbird.

As Courtney dabbed drops of her perfume, she inhaled the flowery jasmine scent. A tiny bottle of perfume with a similar scent was her mother's Christmas gift to Courtney when Courtney had turned seventeen, a rare treat Mom had to hide from Dad.

Lowell's favorite scent was sweet pea, so he'd given her perfumes and body sprays with that scent. Even his nickname for her was Sweet Pea. For some time, she'd found the gesture, the perfume, and the moniker as sweet as their names. But when she'd wanted to change back to a jasmine fragrance and he hadn't let her, the sweet-pea scent had become suffocating and after some time even nauseating. Then she'd realized his nickname for her didn't mean he'd found her sweet but that he'd found her small and insignificant.

One of the first things she'd done after leaving him was buy a tiny bottle of jasmine-scented body spray since she couldn't afford perfumes at the time. She'd had to go hungry that day, but it had been worth it.

Once again, it wasn't about her right now. It was about her little girl's well-being. Just the thought squeezed Courtney's heart as she reached her bedroom door on crutches.

Hmm, how could she get to the kitchen without making any noise? The bedroom was carpeted, so it muffled the sound of crutches, but the hall floor was hardwood. Should she just hop there while carrying the crutches? She twisted the doorknob and opened the door, and the aroma of fresh-brewed coffee reached her nostrils, joined by the scent of fresh-baked bread.

Was Sean up already? Her heart perked up, though it shouldn't. As if reading her thoughts, he stepped out of the kitchen and walked into the hall with a steaming mug in his hand. He smiled at her. "I hope I didn't wake you up."

"You didn't. I couldn't sleep." She clomped toward him, not worrying anymore about the staccato of the rubber-footed crutches against the wood. She did worry about the staccato of her pulse in his presence. Then again, she had much more significant things to worry about.

Ada trotted into the hall and nudged Courtney with her cold nose once she reached her.

"Good morning, darling." Courtney leaned toward the dog and stroked her silky back, glad one of the first things she saw in the morning was the pet. After seeing Sean, of course.

Ada licked Courtney's hand, the tongue rough against Courtney's skin.

"Sorry to hear about the sleepless night." His brown eyes darkened. "I took the liberty of making an omelet and putting biscuits in the oven. I'll get you a cup of coffee if you like."

Something inside her shifted. Nobody had ever made breakfast for her, not since she'd been little. She'd done it for other people and had often been treated like a servant. She'd even had to make breakfast for her sister and herself after she learned to operate the stove. After all, it had only been fair to return a favor for babysitting.

Having someone now make this kind gesture meant so much.

How was it possible Sean could ground her and make her feel like she could fly, even while worry weighed down on her more than ever, even while she couldn't *walk* on her own?

Some women dreamed of diamonds. She dreamed of a breakfast together she didn't have to make.

"Thank you. My stomach is too queasy for breakfast. But I'd love some coffee." She stepped through the hall near him, catching a whiff of his now so familiar and dear scent of hay and leather. She stilled, breathing it in, holding it in for later when she'd have to live without him.

In the kitchen, she washed her hands with a new liquid hand soap, catching a faint hint of jasmine.

"Are you okay?" He pulled out a chair for her in the knotty-pine breakfast nook. "Um, probably not a good question. How are you holding up? Is it okay if I just bring coffee here?"

"I'd appreciate it." She only answered one question, the easy one, because she didn't know how to answer the others. "Should I help feed Ada or change her water?"

"I already did both. Took her for an early walk, too."

The normalcy of the scene slammed into her with a force she didn't expect, maybe because her defenses were bare after the sleepless night and the mountain of worries and insurmountable hope about Lark. As much as she loved being in the sky and the freedom it had given her after years of being controlled, was it possible she again craved the domestic scene of sharing a family meal? One would think Lowell had beaten it out of her.

Yet as Sean brought her a mug of coffee and a heaping plate with omelet and biscuits—saying "just in case you change your mind"—it was the most romantic gesture ever. Well, after his eagerness to help her search for her daughter, of course.

Ada walked toward the breakfast nook, her toenails clicking against hardwood, then stretched out on the floor not far from the table.

Courtney's fingers tightened around the warm mug, and she breathed in its aroma, then sipped some. Why did coffee taste a million times better when someone else—someone who cared about her—made it?

Huh. She'd better channel her thoughts in the right direction. "Any news about Lowell or Naomi?"

A muscle moved in Sean's jaw as if he didn't want to disappoint her. He scooped a forkful of his omelet. "Not yet. But it's still early."

Her heart sank, but he was right. It was early, and she couldn't ask Paisley, Jessie, or Ronan to pull an all-nighter. It was extremely kind of them to be helping to start with. Courtney would have to be patient, though she didn't know how to do that when it came to her daughter.

She sipped more flavorful coffee, then put the mug on the table, covering a knot in the pine that peered at her like a target. Her fingers seemed to move toward Sean's on their own accord. She stopped them with an effort.

Why couldn't she have met him first instead of Lowell? Sean would be so easy to fall in love with. She was more than halfway there already. He'd treat her sister and mother with respect instead of finding fault with them and making Courtney push them away. He'd make a wonderful husband, way beyond her wildest dreams. And he'd make a great dad, nothing like her own father.

Nothing like Lowell, either, if her suspicions were correct and he'd kidnapped her baby, then pawned the child off on someone else, which her mind still couldn't fully comprehend. Could he ever love anyone else besides himself?

Or could it be that if she'd met someone like Sean in high school, she'd have walked past him? Two guys who'd seemed nice had asked her out after she'd met Lowell. She'd said no because she'd been taken by him already.

Sean hadn't told her a hundred compliments a minute, hadn't given her lavish gifts, hadn't reminded her how grateful she should be that he'd chosen her like Lowell had been quick to do in the beginning of their relationship. Sean's kindness was quiet and meaningful, and he didn't talk himself up, while Lowell's fake affection had been so flashy it had blinded her for years.

To the point she'd never fully realized he'd loathed having a baby with her so much that he'd go to unspeakable lengths. Her heart shattered for the thousandth time, after she'd thought there was nothing left to shatter.

"If we find Lowell, you won't be running to him, right? At least, not alone." Sean placed a half-eaten biscuit on his plate and searched her eyes.

"Right." She wouldn't be *running* to Lowell. She'd be *flying* to him. She couldn't put Sean in danger.

The German shepherd got up and ran to the living room. Strangely enough, Courtney missed the pet's quiet presence. How much more would she miss Sean when she had to leave? The next moment, Ada rushed back with a toy in her teeth. She placed the toy at Courtney's feet.

Courtney looked up at Sean. "Is she... is she trying to comfort me?"

The corners of his delectable mouth moved up a little. Delectable? What was she thinking? "I think so."

Wow. She leaned to pet the dog. "In your family, even the dogs are considerate."

"Maybe, but you seem to have forgotten our cat." He must've noticed her wince because he hurried to add, "I'm joking. Obviously. And obviously, not very successfully." He gestured at the plate. "I understand you don't have any appetite. But, um, you need to maintain your strength."

Ada lifted her head and barked as if giving her vote, as well.

Courtney had often made delicious dinners for Lowell, but he'd shown up late after a night out with friends, and she'd have to put his food in the trash. She didn't want to behave like that toward Sean.

And he had a point. She needed to maintain her strength if she wanted to be any good for Lark. "True. And thank you so much for making breakfast." She managed a few bites of eggs with green peppers, onions, and ham, and surprisingly, her stomach didn't protest the new arrivals.

Self-reproach stung her. After all, how could she enjoy the food and the company when she still knew nothing about her little girl?

"There's nothing we can do right now but wait." Again, he seemed to read her mind. "As soon as my family has anything, they'll let us know."

"Yes. It's just..." Her throat clogged up. She stared into her coffee.

"It's difficult. I understand."

I understand.

His words reverberated through her and settled inside like the treasure they were.

She'd never been as loquacious as Lowell, never been a talker at all, and sometimes it had irritated Lowell. She'd had difficulty explaining herself because, even when she'd done her best, it hadn't seemed to matter to her parents or her former husband. They'd never understood her or claimed they never did. Even with her friends and her sister, it had been difficult once Courtney had started taking an interest in car parts to placate her father. The fashion trends and boy bands her girl circle liked had little significance to Courtney while her family struggled to survive. And she'd learned fast enough that people didn't like hearing about other people's problems.

Maybe one of the reasons she'd ended up working as a pilot had been that it was easier for her to communicate with machines than with people. Before, she'd never truly felt heard or understood, except in the early stage of Lowell's courtship, and she'd later realized that had all been a pretense on his part.

With Sean, she didn't even need to explain. He somehow understood everything without words. Corny or not, his brown eyes seemed to see straight into her soul, and to her surprise, he seemed to like what he saw. With other people, she'd felt like she'd needed to work hard to earn their mercy, much less their understanding. It was like she'd lived across a river from them, and it had been her responsibility to build the bridge toward them. That bridge she'd so painstakingly created had always ended up being built from glass, and they'd always shattered it with a few stones.

With Sean, the bridge to his attention, respect, and understanding had been erected already. She'd had to make zero effort to create it. The only thing she'd needed to do was to step on it.

She had never before found such a connection to another human being. Her heart ached that she'd have to sever the connection soon. She managed to push down a few more bites of eggs, then bit by bit forced a biscuit around the lump in her throat.

"I wish I could help more." He brushed the back of his hand against her cheek.

It sent a wave of pleasure she shouldn't be feeling, and it took all her willpower not to lean into his touch. "You help by simply being here." It was true.

Ada voiced her opinion again by barking, and Courtney sent her a sad smile. "You, too."

After breakfast and its cleanup, they walked to the living room, festive with golden and silvery garlands adorning the walls. Those, plus the tree with its many ornaments and twinkling lights, left a bittersweet taste in Courtney's mouth. And the stockings above the fireplace mantel, including one with her name, tugged at her heart.

She'd already started imagining spending Christmas at this place. Sean had invited her. But now she didn't know what was going to happen. The happy sight seemed to mock her angst and apprehension. She lowered herself onto the sofa and placed the crutches aside.

Ada jogged to Courtney, then nuzzled her head on Courtney's lap as if in silent support. Courtney rubbed the pet's back, her mind searching for any clue how to find Lark. Then she hugged the flamingo-hued pillow and leaned against the sofa's back, her gaze fixed on the twinkling golden lights.

"I hope and pray your daughter is alive and well and we can find her." Sean sat near her and covered her hand with his. "If we do, what are you going to do next?"

He didn't have to say Lowell would use Lark as leverage. It was surprising he'd waited this long, which might mean he'd made it all up. That meant Lark wasn't alive.

The yummy breakfast seemed to sour in her stomach. "If she was adopted by some miracle and leads a happy life, I'll step away. Honest. I'd never want to harm her."

His fingers curled over hers. "I believe you."

"But if not... If she's with Lowell now and he treats her badly..." Something crumpled in her. "I have no clue what I'm going to do. Just that I'll do everything to help her."

As if sensing Courtney's growing distress, Ada licked Courtney's free hand. "Thanks, Ada."

Many more things were breaking her heart. "My daughter would be a stranger to me," she said without looking at him. "And if she's in a good environment, it would have to stay that way. I'll have to let her be. I just want to know she's okay." Then her gaze moved to him. "And if not... How am I going to explain that I'm her mother?"

"You'll be the best mom in the world."

Lowell had told her a million compliments in the beginning, none of which he'd probably meant. But not a single one of them imprinted itself on her as much as Sean's words right now.

"Thank you." She touched his hand with her fingertips, then withdrew when something akin to an electric current—but a good one—went through her. Even in her deeply emotional state or maybe because of it, this rugged cowboy affected her on a level Lowell never could. She was falling for him, and she couldn't let it happen.

She lifted her gaze. "What if we can't find her?" She couldn't imagine living the rest of her life with this uncertainty.

He snatched her hand in both of his. "We will. You'll see."

"How can you be so sure?"

Before he had a chance to answer, Ada rushed to the hall. A motor outside made Courtney tense, though, surely, if someone passed the gate without calling them, that someone had the security code. Every nerve in her body was stretched to the limit, and then they passed that limit.

A minute later, the doorbell rang. Ada barked, but it was a friendly, nonthreatening bark. By then, Courtney had pulled up the camera feed on her phone, and she relaxed somewhat when Paisley showed up on the camera observing the porch.

"I'll open the door." Sean was already on his way.

"Thanks. It's Paisley." Courtney leaned on her crutches as she wobbled after him.

Once Paisley stepped inside, Courtney did her best to read the quirky computer whiz's facial expression, apprehension tightening Courtney's rib cage. Was there any good news? If so, what would it be?

Ada jumped, nearly making the petite woman fall, and she hugged the dog tenderly. "I'm glad to see you, too. Good morning, Sean, Courtney." Sean's sister-in-law released the dog and straightened, her pensive gaze not giving anything away while he helped her out of a ballerina-slipper-hued coat. She stepped out of matching cowboy boots, and the little silver bells attached to them jingled.

Once again, Paisley was a sight to be seen in a yellow-and-black striped sweater and a matching skirt that reached her knees, plus leggings with magical sunrise-toned flowers. A headband with identical flowers propped up her spectacular pink-blue hair. She looked like a giant bumblebee among a field of flowers.

In other times, this sight would've made Courtney smile. But now tension gripped her heart. "Um, anything about Naomi? Or Lowell? You're here, so there must be some news, right?"

"No. I just smelled coffee from a distance." Then Paisley smiled apologetically. "Yes, there's some news."

"How about we discuss it over a cup of that coffee?" Sean gestured toward the breakfast nook.

Courtney almost glared at him, desperate to hear the news right this moment instead of waiting even a second.

Sean made a cup of coffee for Paisley and a new one for Courtney, then brought them to the table. He pulled out their chairs just in time for Courtney to slump onto one because her knees wobbled. She arched her shoulders back and gritted her teeth. She had to pull herself together.

The three of them settled at the breakfast nook, and Ada brought her toy to join them as she stretched out on the hardwood floor under the table. Courtney peered at Paisley as if Courtney's life depended on it.

Paisley cradled the steaming coffee cup. "I believe I found Naomi Bricker." She tapped open a social media account on her phone and showed Courtney the screen. "Is that her?"

The woman in the photo had blonde hair instead of the hazelnut-brown she'd worn when Courtney met her. But Courtney recognized the facial features because they were embedded in her memory forever.

"Yes!" Her heart nearly stopped beating, then restarted with a wild force. "How? Where?" The answer to those questions didn't matter as much as the next one. "Can I go to talk to her?"

Paisley shook her head, her mouth twisting downward. "No."

Courtney's jaw slackened, and she sucked in a sharp breath at the sucker punch. "You're not going to tell me how and where to find her?"

"I mean you won't be able to go talk to Naomi. She went by a different name, but that's not the issue here." Paisley took a small sip of her coffee, a placating expression in her eyes.

Determination boiled Courtney's blood, and she snatched her crutches, then leaped to her feet—or a foot and a crutch in this case. She didn't care that her untouched cup rattled and her coffee sloshed over its brim. Ada jumped to her paws, as well. "Even if she lives in Antarctica, I know of a pilot who can fly me there. Once there, I'll talk to penguins to get directions if I have to."

"It's not that. I'm sorry." Something about Paisley's soft words made Courtney plop back in the chair. Then it registered. Paisley had said Naomi Bricker "*went* by a different name." Past tense.

Courtney's heart sank, and her hopes drowned in the coffee in front of her. "Did she...?" Courtney didn't want to say the words as if that would make them true.

Sean reached for her hand.

"I'm sorry," Paisley repeated again.

Ada lay on the floor again and tilted her head as if confused and not understanding if they were coming or going. Courtney knew just the feeling.

"Wait. N–no. It's not possible." But as Courtney stuttered, Paisley merely looked at her. Didn't she understand? "How do you know it's not another ruse? After all, if this woman faked my daughter's death, couldn't she have faked her own?"

"I initially wondered the same, but no. This was real."

Her hopes crushed, but Courtney couldn't let it bring her down. Not if her daughter needed her.

"What about Lowell?" Courtney had checked her email on her phone several times throughout the long night. There were no new emails from him.

What if a new email came while she'd talked to Sean? Impatient, she fished her phone out of her jeans back pocket, and then the sleek smooth phone almost slipped from her hands. Sean caught it before it landed in her cup of coffee. Ada jumped to catch it, as well, but thankfully her teeth only clasped air a safe distance away.

"Here we go." He handed back the phone.

She took it with more caution. "Thanks."

"There aren't any new emails from Lowell. I checked while on the porch." Paisley's grip tightened on her cup, and she drank some coffee as if to give herself time to think of a careful answer. "I'm narrowing down his location. Someone helped him cover his tracks. If that was him, of course."

It had to be. Or not? Was Courtney naïve again, this time falling for some scam? Was her hope Lark was alive just Courtney's crutch to lean on because of her broken heart?

"Okay. Okay." She rubbed her temples. "But you found some information about Naomi that could be useful, right?" For simplicity, she used the name she was used to calling the midwife.

"Right. And I've passed the info to Jessie and her husband. They'll use their connections to get more information. Here's what I found out so far. Naomi had experience as a midwife. She also worked at a hospital, though not the one she claimed. She had social media accounts but wasn't very active on them. She was divorced twice and had no children in either of the marriages. She was survived by two older brothers. She had a dog, and one of her brothers took in the dog."

"What about Naomi's close friends? Maybe she confided in them about what she did?" The chances of that were slim to none, but still higher than penguins giving directions.

"I'm sifting through her friends' profiles."

Right. Paisley needed to sleep, as well. She must've gotten up early as it was to work on the computer.

Sean leaned forward. "Paisley, you said she didn't have children... Did that mean, um...?"

"Based on online groups she was in, I don't think she could have children."

Courtney's thoughts jumped around frantically. "Maybe this motivated her for the entire charade? To get Lark?" Again, she was jumping to conclusions.

"I didn't see her posting any photos online of a little girl." Paisley drained her coffee. "But obviously, she'd have an important reason not to if our suspicions are right."

Paisley hadn't said "*your* suspicions," and it warmed Courtney, as did the woman's eagerness to help. In other times, maybe they could be friends. Lowell had made Courtney eliminate her friends, but she wasn't under his thumb any longer.

Of course, if she had to leave this place soon, most likely without saying goodbye, Sean and his family wouldn't look on her so favorably.

Later in the day, Paisley sent Lowell's location, which turned out to be on a Caribbean Island.

Courtney also received an email that made her gasp. It was from the same email address, and it had several photos. Two were of a baby and two of a toddler near a Christmas tree. She stared at the photos hungrily and took in everything. This was her daughter. It had to be.

Her world shook. As soon as she came out of her stupor, with trembling fingers she started researching airline tickets. Sean wouldn't want her to put her life in danger, but she had to do this. An overwhelming need to see Lark, to make sure she was all right swept Courtney up and steeled her weak resolve that wobbled when she thought of Sean.

She had no clue how she'd manage to get to the airport unnoticed, especially on crutches. She could hop or crawl through the hall, but what next? And what would she do once she reached the island? How would she find Lowell? She needed Sean more than ever, but she couldn't talk to him about this.

By some miracle, she managed to book a one-way ticket for one person. Someone must've canceled at the last minute. Pain erupted inside her already. She'd have to leave in the middle of the night in secret, somehow make it outside the gate without waking Sean, and meet a taxi there. Knife-sharp pain sliced through her. Sean would never forgive her for this betrayal.

She didn't want to break his heart, but what choice did she have?

Chapter Eleven

Early the next morning, Sean tiptoed to the kitchen. He did his best to move as quietly as possible. It was difficult to see in the darkness, but he didn't want to wake Courtney, so he didn't flip the switch in the hall.

His heart constricted. Courtney had looked so stricken yesterday. It had taken all his willpower not to gather her into his arms and keep her there. He shouldn't be pining for her, especially considering the circumstances. But based on how his heart ached, he was way too far gone already.

The next moment he realized that he wasn't alone. He froze in place, and his body tensed up. Then he identified the sound as Ada's nails clicking against the hardwood floor.

He flipped the kitchen switch, blinked at the light, and looked at the German shepherd who followed him there. "Why are you up so early?" he mouthed.

Thankfully, Ada didn't bark and just tilted her head as if asking, "No. Why are *you* up so early?"

"I wanted to make coffee and breakfast for myself." Why was he talking to the dog? He put out kibble and fresh water for her.

Dogs couldn't roll their eyes, but if they could, that would likely be her expression. As it was, she just stared at him in exasperation as if saying, "Who are you kidding? Certainly not me."

"Fine," he muttered. "I wanted to make coffee and breakfast for Courtney."

Ada ran to him, then rushed into the dark hall. He followed her silhouette and found her standing near Courtney's door. Ada let out a low whine.

He pressed a finger to his lips as if even dogs could understand *that* gesture. "Shh." He kept his voice low. "I miss her, too, but let's not wake her up."

Never mind that everything in him wanted to see Courtney soon. But she needed some rest. Most likely, she hadn't been able to sleep after getting the news about Lowell. Sean sent up a prayer for her.

Later today, they'd have to decide as a family which of them would go close to Lowell. Worry tightened his lungs. All the roads to find Lark led through Lowell, and now they could better pinpoint his location thanks to Paisley. But just the thought of Courtney going anywhere near the man who'd harmed her so much sent a shiver down Sean's spine.

Courtney was safe here. She wouldn't be safe if she left the lodge. On the other hand, he'd never keep her in a bulletproof cage.

As if not getting the message, Ada sat near the yellow room's door.

Sean shook his head at the dog, though his heart stirred, not getting the message, either. He couldn't wait to see Courtney. "It's great that you want to guard her sleep. But I'm afraid to leave you here in case you start barking."

Ada tilted her head as if asking, "Who do you think I am?"

"A dog. Who could bark if a squirrel runs outside."

Just great. He was having an imaginary conversation with a pet.

"Heel," he whispered as he strode to the kitchen again to make breakfast.

When no sound of nails on the wood clicked behind him, he turned around. Ada hadn't moved.

"Ada, heel." He patted his thigh, keeping his voice low.

The German shepherd walked to him, but then she turned around and rushed to the front door.

Sean tensed. Did she sense someone outside? His senses on high alert, he checked the camera footage on his phone. Everything seemed calm. So he leaned to Ada. "Do you need to go for a walk?"

Hmm. She'd usually bring a leash if so, and this time, she didn't. Maybe she just wanted to run outside? He opened the front door, but as frosty air rushed inside, the dog didn't rush outside.

Sean ran his fingers through his hair. "What is it with you today?"

He closed and locked the door because she seemed to change her mind again and trotted to the living room now. But she looked back as if to make sure he followed her. He switched on the living room light while she growled.

"Come on, Ada. No growling. We don't want to wake—" He'd turned around and noticed a sheet of paper on the coffee table near which Ada was baring teeth.

His stomach slipped into the carpet in premonition. He picked up what turned out to be a folded letter.

The words danced in front of his eyes as he unfolded it.

Dear Sean,

I'm doing this with a heavy heart, but I hope you'll understand one day. I need to know for sure that my daughter is alive, and if so, I need to find her. Even thinking of meeting Lowell again terrifies me. But that's the only way to ever see Lark.

You've been wonderful to me. You're by far the best thing that ever happened to me. I'm still breathing thanks to you. I realize that, after I repay you horribly by sneaking out, you might never want to see me again. I am sorry I disappointed you and your family. Please tell them I am very, very sorry.

I'll never forget their kindness. I'll never forget you.

Courtney.

The paper slipped to the carpet with a quiet whoosh. Déjà vu enveloped him. Now he understood what Genevieve felt when her daughter left the safety of the lodge and went to meet her biological father, which had meant a disaster for her.

Ada hung her head as if apologizing that she didn't bark.

"Not your fault, Ada. How... Why... Doesn't she understand...?" He dashed to the garage. His truck was still there.

With worry slamming him so hard he could barely breathe, he brought out his phone and checked flights to the islands where Lowell was supposed to be. The next one was leaving in two hours. No tickets available, of course.

His heart racing, he dashed to his room, threw some clothes into a duffel bag, then picked up his outerwear in the hall. He dropped the duffel bag and pulled on the boots. "Sorry, Ada, I'll have to go. I'll ask Cormac to take care of you."

The dog barked.

"I wish I could take you on the plane. But I have no idea how *I'll* get on the plane myself." He snatched his coat and scarf but didn't waste time putting them on. He sprinted into the garage, jumped into the truck, and revved the engine.

It was dark as he drove through the gate. He'd imagined and dreaded Courtney eventually flying away from him. But not like this.

Lord, please help me get on that plane in time. Please keep her safe.

He floored the accelerator on the gravel road covered in fresh snow. The truck growled in protest but dashed forward.

How did she even manage to leave? In snow. Without a vehicle. On crutches. She must've walked outside the gate to make sure she didn't wake him up and had a taxi pick her up there.

His jaw set tight, and he called Paisley on the hands-free phone and relayed the situation.

Like he'd expected, she spurred into action immediately. "I'll try to find out if Courtney's name is on the flight as a passenger. I'll see what I can do about getting you on that flight if she's there. It's the most difficult time of the year to try to get airline tickets, though."

He groaned. "I know! I mean, thank you."

Why couldn't Courtney just talk to him? Disappointment sliced through him. He slowed as he made a turn from the country road to the main one, then pressed on the gas pedal again. At such an early hour, outside the town limits, the road was deserted.

Paisley's perky voice filled the vehicle cabin again. "I'll let the rest of the family know, okay? We have two cops in the family. I'm sure they'll volunteer to go with you. Well, most likely on the next flight because even I won't be able to get three tickets on a plane leaving in two hours." Then tenderness coated her voice. "I'm sure my husband will volunteer, too."

Gratitude spread through him. How did he manage to get such an amazing family, both his blood relatives and those newly added by marriage? Then he said, "I'd rather he stay with you." He didn't say it was because Paisley was pregnant and might need her husband's help and support, but he didn't need to. "I do appreciate the help."

"No problem." She paused as if unsure what to say next. "I, um, I imagine you're upset with Courtney right now. But she doesn't know you the way we do. She lived with a controlling and abusive father, then with a controlling and abusive husband. She must've been afraid you wouldn't let her go. And... well, I haven't given birth yet, but I'd risk my life for this baby already. So Courtney is ready to put her life on the line for her child. But she probably doesn't feel she has the right to put other people's lives on the line for her cause."

His fingers tightened around the steering wheel to the point that his knuckles whitened. He couldn't let Courtney get hurt again.

Ever.

Chapter Twelve

Courtney sank into the airplane seat and wished she could sink through the floor, as well. A mountain weighed on her shoulders.

Traveling with crutches and a casted leg was also far from ideal, even if she was just a passenger and paid for a seat with extra legroom. She stretched her leg carefully and turned to the closed window as passengers buzzed around her, placing luggage and taking seats.

Her entire being missed Sean already, and she felt empty like the seat near her. Everything in her protested her reckless decision and wanted to rush back to the safety of his arms. Longing for him unraveled like a powerful current in the ocean waters above which they'd be flying soon, pulling her in with it.

No, this wouldn't do. She needed to concentrate on finding her daughter. She had to make sure Lark was all right and do everything to help her if she wasn't, though of course, Lowell wouldn't give up either one of them without a fight. She shuddered. Was she ready for this? Was she going to survive this new encounter? Finding her little songbird was the priority and not Courtney's heart that might be breaking.

Then more crushing weight made her grind her teeth in her struggle not to let it bow her under. How could she do this to Sean, sneak off in the middle of the night? She'd understand if he never forgave her, though her insides started aching at the thought.

But it was for his own good. The mess she was in now was of her making, and it was up to her to figure this out. And while she needed his support now more than ever, if there was even a remote chance she'd put him in danger, she couldn't risk it.

She'd made a mistake by sneaking away, yes, but it was a mistake she had to make for both Sean's and Lark's sakes.

Grimacing, Courtney clicked the seat belt closed, and her fingers hovered over the cold smooth metal. She groaned. She couldn't deny a selfish reason for sneaking out. Seeing Sean by her side would aggravate Lowell. He had a jealous streak, though she'd never been allowed to have one and question his whereabouts when he'd shown up late at night.

She flinched. How was she falling into the same trap again? She'd spent the biggest part of her marriage trying so hard not to make him angry. Just like her mother with Courtney's dad. Instead of learning from her mother's mistakes, Courtney had inherited that way of thinking.

Her stomach clenched, and if not for her seat, she'd shift back as if to defend herself. She'd thought she'd changed. Apparently not. More weight piled up. Feeling trapped and lost, she nearly jumped to her feet to leave the plane. But the seat belt pulled her back.

No.

She couldn't miss the chance to find her little girl. What if Lark was suffering in Lowell's care or in the care of whomever he'd hired or manipulated into watching over her?

What was next? Courtney rubbed her temples, throbbing after a sleepless night, and her nose followed a passenger carrying a cup of coffee as if just a sniff could boost her energy. How would she search for her songbird once she got to the Caribbean Island where Lowell might be? She'd have to figure it out there. At least, she'd managed to get the ticket on such short notice, especially considering it was just over a week before Christmas. The busiest travel time for the year.

Her most profitable time of the year, too, but that couldn't be helped. She'd already been grounded as a pilot until she healed. She clenched her teeth, then forced herself to unclench them as a young slim woman with two blonde braids, dressed in an apple-red coat, smiled at her from an opposite seat. It wouldn't do to scowl at people.

Missed season or not, Courtney could provide for herself and her daughter now. Unlike when she'd depended on Lowell for pure survival or had thought she did.

A middle-aged bearded man in a beanie and smelling of cigarettes took a seat near her without sparing her a glance. She tensed in close proximity to a man, then relaxed her muscles. Not every man was a threat.

"We should be taking off soon, right?" The guy popped a stick of gum in his mouth. The mint scent helped with the cigarette odor, but not much.

"Right." Adrenaline infused her veins. Being a passenger was a far cry from being a pilot. Still, she'd be in the sky soon. And miles closer to her daughter. Her heart soared.

And miles away from Sean. Her heart dipped like a plane midflight when the engines—all of them—stopped working. She'd probably ruined her minuscule chance with him, if there'd ever been any.

"Would you mind trading seats with me, please?" Sean's voice made her head whip up. "This is my friend, and I'd appreciate it so much if I could spend the flight with her."

Was she imagining things?

The guy near her squirmed. "I paid for extra leg space."

"I'll be glad to recompense for it and double for the inconvenience." Sean kept his voice polite but firm.

That did the trick. The bearded man unclicked his seat belt. "I'll be happy to help."

After passing over a wad of cash, Sean sat beside her.

Her pulse quickened in his mere presence, but remorse was louder than attraction. "That was... smooth." Not the best words she could find.

"Declan would be proud." Sean's voice didn't have its usual warmth now.

She couldn't blame him. "I'm sorry I sneaked out without letting you know."

The pilot announced takeoff.

Sean rubbed his forehead. "I understand your reasons. I just... I just don't want history to repeat itself."

She tensed again as if a blow was coming her way already. "Me, either. How did you figure out I'd be on this flight?"

The plane shook a little, gathered together like a bird about to take wing, then moved forward. A part of her wished she was in the pilots' cabin. She pulled up the window blind and looked at the runway bathed in morning mist. The sun was rising. Could she hope for a sunrise in her life?

Being here near him gave her a feeling of exhilaration, as well, and that was saying something. Her gaze moved to him. He held it. He'd soon hold her heart if she wasn't careful. Or maybe he did already, and she just didn't want to admit it.

"It wasn't difficult to guess where you'd be going once Paisley gave us the IP address location." He studied her.

She might as well admit it. "I'm glad you're here." Then she grimaced, knowing she'd have to ruin whatever connection was building between them again. "You can't accompany me when I go to Lowell, though."

He didn't argue. "We'll figure something out."

We.

She liked the sound of that. Lots of emotion must be playing in her eyes now, so she turned away and looked again at the lit runaway, wishing her path was just as clear. She could find her way in the sky but not in her life. Why?

Usually, the anticipation of a plane taking flight would uncurl in her belly, and it did, especially when it went airborne like now. But this time, the sheer panic of a possible confrontation with Lowell overshadowed it. She'd never truly confronted him. Well, she had to when he'd shown up at her place this year, but before, she'd just fled.

Just like she'd fled from Sean last night. Her stomach clenched. It wasn't just about protecting him. She hadn't wanted a confrontation, knowing he wouldn't want her to go to Lowell.

Was it engraved in her since childhood to avoid conflict to survive?

There was another fear, as well. Lark wouldn't even know who Courtney was, and it'd break a mother's heart.

"I'm going to be a stranger to my daughter," she whispered.

"Once she gets to know you, she'll love you." His voice softened.

He didn't say, "*If* she gets to know you."

His words softened something in her core. After her divorce, she'd had to construct a shell around her heart like the airplane's, but with Sean, it was becoming as soft and gentle as a bird's feathers.

Her hand moved toward his, but she stopped it. "I deceived you. And yet you're still kind to me. I don't understand it. Why are you not upset?"

"Would you want me to be upset?"

"Well, no, but..."

"Okay, I'm angry. And disappointed. And yes, upset."

"I get the point." Be careful what you wish for. She suppressed a grimace. She'd asked for it, hadn't she? She had no one to blame but herself.

Look what you made me do.

She shook her head, desperate to forget the words Lowell told her so many times. This was a different situation. A different measure of culpability. A different man.

"But you matter more than that anger," Sean said. "And I understand the reasons for your actions."

To be understood and to be supported. Wasn't that what a lot of people looked for and some never found? Had *she* found it? Only to have to walk away from it.

She sighed. "Was it naïve of me to rush into this? I mean, how are we going to find him? I heard islanders spot outsiders quickly. But it's a large island. And they might not reveal that information because we're outsiders, as well."

He placed his hand on hers where it rested over the chair arm dividing them, making warmth spread through her. "Paisley is working on it."

Courtney blinked. "I thought nothing about that woman could surprise me anymore, and you just proved me wrong. If you're okay to share, how *exactly* is she working on it?"

"She's been running a project to help abused people escape for a while. As a result, she assembled an encrypted database of many people who volunteer to help. Some of them simply believe in the cause, and some are former abuse survivors. Many are friends and family of survivors." He glanced at her, compassion in his eyes.

She turned away and stared at the clouds. She'd always loved flying above the clouds. But apparently, she'd also had her head in the clouds for a long part of her marriage, believing Lowell would change.

She tried on the word *survivor*, and it fit as if tailored to her. Why hadn't she looked at herself as a survivor before? First, she'd considered herself someone to blame. Basically, a scapegoat. Sometimes, she'd thought of herself as a victim. It had taken so long to rebuild her self-esteem, to reconstruct her identity from nothing. Being a survivor sounded much better.

Sean continued, "Basically, she now has a worldwide network of people she can contact if needed."

"Wow." She turned back to him. "Even in the Caribbean Islands?"

His lips curved up. "You'd be surprised."

She lifted her gaze from those lips because she shouldn't be thinking about kissing him. But that half smile told her he might've forgiven her already. Her insides warmed. In the past, it had taken her groveling and begging to be forgiven for things she hadn't even done. On the contrary, Sean easily forgave things she *had* done.

"Paisley is an inspiration." While Courtney sometimes felt like a disappointment, maybe because she'd been told she was a disappointment so many times. She'd only learned to feel differently when she learned to fly, in many senses. Well, she could fly right now, but not the way she wanted.

"She is an inspiration, indeed. So are you."

Her heart beating faster, she got lost in his dark eyes again. But it wasn't even that. As she looked at her reflection in his pupils, she saw admiration in his eyes while she'd found contempt in Lowell's.

Her heart stuttered, and she leaned toward him as much as the seat belt allowed. Then she unbuckled her seat belt because the sign allowed it anyway. And yes, because she wanted to be closer to Sean.

"I wish you could see yourself with my eyes." His voice thickened. "Then you'd see how amazing you are."

She wished that, too. Maybe if she stared into his eyes long enough, she'd be able to. It was an incredible—and unusual—feeling when someone believed in you.

That wasn't the only reason she was drawn to him, but it was one of the important ones.

"Thank you. It means a lot to me." On impulse, she leaned toward him to kiss his cheek in gratitude.

But he turned closer to her at the same moment, and her lips ended up brushing against his lips rather than his cheek.

Blood rushed faster in her veins, and her breathing quickened. Her pulse seemed to become a staccato, and everything around her went hazy. She didn't hear people talking anymore or the plane's engines or the polite flight attendant asking passengers what they'd like to drink. She only heard her heart beating. Or was it Sean's?

She realized her mistake, of course, and she should've pulled back. Instead, she deepened the kiss, and he responded, sending her into a new whirlwind of sensations. Who needed mistletoe as an excuse, when the simple touch of Sean's lips could make her feel so much?

She was floating in the air, not because of the airplane but because of the way he made her feel. Euphoria buoyed her every cell, leaving her light as a feather. Pleasant sensations spread through her. She didn't want the kiss to stop, but she managed to pull herself away.

She touched her lips as if to keep the sensations there a few precious moments longer. But she was sending him mixed messages again. And she couldn't let her sweeping attraction to a man dictate her actions. "That..." she started.

"Was incredible," he finished for her.

"Shouldn't have happened," she said at the same time.

His eyes, so caring and passionate, hardened. "Please don't say you're sorry."

She wasn't sorry. This was the man she wanted to kiss again and again. This was the man she wanted to love. This was even the man she wanted to marry.

But hadn't she done it all with someone who also seemed to care about her? And hadn't it ended in disaster?

She should be thinking about her daughter instead of kissing a man she might have to leave soon. The exhilaration of floating in the sky evaporated, and worry and heartache hit her as if she struck the land without a parachute. Not that she'd know how it felt, but she'd imagined it would be about as painful.

The pretty flight attendant with wavy chestnut-brown hair and an upturned nose passed the drinks. The coffee aroma drifted to Courtney.

"Coffee, please," Courtney said when it was her turn.

She'd need an extra energy boost after a sleepless night. Then she sipped her hot drink—the coffee Sean made for her was way better—and tried to gather her wayward thoughts after that incredible kiss. But everything in her wanted to experience those pleasant sensations again, and trying to think rationally was like flying through turbulence.

Once the perky flight attendant was out of earshot, Courtney turned to Sean again. The disappointment in his features broke her heart, but she steeled her resolve. "We don't have much time left, and we need to discuss a lot of things. Can you tell me more about that islander who's going to help us?"

Sean drained his water and placed the cup on the tray. "Her name is Tamara. We usually don't ask for the last name. She's the sister of a survivor Paisley helped. Tamara is a single mom, so that might be another reason she volunteered to help you. She's in the IT field, and her job is fully remote. So three years ago, she relocated herself and her little daughter to this island where a few of her coworkers lived. She helped her sister relocate there, as well."

"Got it. Thanks." Something shifted inside Courtney. Another pain, another loss she couldn't forget.

Would her sister do something similar for her if Courtney hadn't pushed her away because of Lowell's lies? She'd have to reach out to her sister and mother again. And keep trying. One didn't need to wait until a new year to make resolutions. Any day was a good day to try to change life for the better.

And fine, Courtney might not ever have the same relationship with her family as Sean did with his, but that didn't mean she should have none at all.

She squared her shoulders and drained her hot black coffee. Lowell had taken so much from her. It was time to claim it all back.

"Lowell told me my sister flirted with him and tried to steal him from me. I–I believed him." Why did she blurt *that* out? How many mistakes had she made in her life? Probably too many to count. "Mom took my sister's side, of course. They stopped talking to me."

Compassion melted his dark eyes again. "I know I said it before, but it's not your fault."

Ducking her head, she fiddled with the seat arm. "Um, please apologize to your family for me. For leaving the way I did."

He shrugged. "You'll be able to talk to Ronan and Jessie in the evening."

She drew invisible lines on the seat arm. "You mean by phone?"

"They are catching the flight after this. We couldn't get two additional seats on this flight. It was a miracle I got a seat. God's providence."

Would God help her get her little girl back? Or had God given up on her like she'd given up on Him?

The generosity of his family members floored her, but... "You shouldn't have asked them."

"I didn't. They volunteered."

"They are amazing." She meant it.

"I know." His voice warmed but then dipped again. "I, well, want to talk about something else. I thought a lot about whether I should say anything about this, and I think I should."

She winced. Was he going to tell her about his feelings for her? While everything in her welcomed the idea, it was such a bad time. And she didn't know how she'd respond. She'd never want to hurt him. But she couldn't be distracted when so much was at stake.

He searched her eyes. "I don't want to crush your hopes. I really don't. But... even if Lowell has a little girl living with him who looks like him, how can you be sure it's your daughter? He lied to you before."

Disappointment slammed her. Not only because he had a point she didn't want to see but also because he wasn't going to talk about his feelings for her. Could she... Did she want him to? How selfish could she be?

"Intuition." She made a cutting gesture with her hand. "I'll feel it."

He didn't say her intuition proved to be wrong before when clouded by her desire to see something that wasn't there. He didn't have to.

"Besides, if the girl is a four-year-old, who else's could she be?" She didn't want to believe Lowell had cheated on her. But he'd often stayed out, showing up in the middle of the night. And sometimes she'd caught a faint whiff of a feminine perfume, but he'd assured her it was only her imagination.

"Maybe, just to be on the safe side, it would be a good idea to compare the girl's DNA with yours."

Her eyes widened. "Is that even possible? I mean without him noticing? I don't want you to break into his house to steal a hairbrush or something."

"Um." He cleared his throat. "I didn't intend to break into his house, but thank you for thinking so highly of me. We'll leave that idea as a last resort."

Heat rose to her cheeks, and she ducked her head. "Oh, okay."

He touched her hand again. "Ronan gave me a DNA kit. We'll think of something. If you're okay sharing the entire story with Tamara, she might come up with something."

Oh how she liked the sound of the word *we*! And then she realized how she'd respond if he confessed his feelings for her. She tightened her fingers around the armrest, wishing it were his hand instead. Deep inside, she knew she had feelings for him, and it scared her and encouraged her at the same time.

"Why don't you try to get some sleep?" His voice softened.

She shook her head. "I'm too wound up to sleep. Besides, I just drank coffee."

Soon, she'd have to confront the man who'd beaten her nearly to death. She could lose her daughter a second time. How could she relax when her life hung in the balance like a plane in a death spiral?

But as her head slipped to his shoulder, all the tension swirling inside lessened somehow, and she drifted off to sleep.

Chapter Thirteen

The bright sunshine reflecting off the ocean contradicted Sean's concern for Courtney. With much warmer weather and vibrant magenta and orange flowers among emerald greenery, it was a different world here from the winter wonderland in the Show Me State. But the tropical sun couldn't melt his worry.

Courtney had covered her eyes with aviator sunglasses and added a gray cap that hid her hair and part of her lovely face, and he suspected that was the point. But the tension in her posture spoke volumes.

He tore his gaze away from her and shook Tamara's extended hand as she met them at the dock. "Great to meet you. Thank you so much for helping us."

"No problem. I owe one to Paisley. Besides, it's beyond horrible when a daughter is taken away from her mother." Tamara's jaw tightened, and she shuddered, perhaps imagining herself in the same situation.

Toned and tanned as if she spent a lot of time outdoors, she looked summer bright in her canary-yellow off-shoulder top, knee-length bleached jean shorts, and pink flip-flops with plastic tropical flowers. The same tropical flowers were painted on her toenails. A high, sun-streaked blonde ponytail poked from an opening in a faded yellow sun visor. But unlike Courtney's cap, Tamara had pushed the brim of hers back to reveal her eyes.

Not for long, though, because then she put on sunglasses. "I'll ferry you on my boat to the next island, which is much smaller than this one."

Uh-oh. This was a new development. Sucking in a deep breath of humid and salty air, Sean exchanged glances with Courtney. "But why?"

Tamara shrugged. "Because that's where the man and the little girl you're looking for are."

Courtney gasped. "You found him? And he *does* have a girl with him?"

"My friend who lives on that island did find him. Which is a good thing because it's much easier to spot an outsider there than here. Way too many tourists here. Not that I can complain about that since I was one of them once."

Courtney's eyes went huge, making him step closer to her. "Are you sure?"

"I sent him the photo, and he recognized it."

Tamara turned around and marched toward a sailboat, clearly expecting them to follow her, which they did.

The ocean breeze ruffled a wisp of dark hair that escaped from under Courtney's cap. She blinked fast as if trying to resist tears. "The little girl... Did she look all right? Happy? Or... was she sad?"

His heart went out to her, and he reached for her hand. Something akin to an electric current, but a pleasant one, went through him. He wanted to offer his support, but he needed this visible connection to her, too, despite a part of him still reeling after her deceit. Didn't she know he'd do anything to help her?

Tamara shrugged again, walking fast in the marina. "She looked content enough to me. Not malnourished. No visible bruises."

Courtney released a whoosh of obvious relief, but then her fingers tightened around his. He understood her dilemma.

What would be in Lark's best interest? He should've talked to someone from Paisley's team of volunteer psychologists. If her songbird was okay with Lowell, if he was a horrible husband but an all-right father, should Courtney find the strength to walk away? Or would Lowell eventually abuse his daughter, as well?

And if so, how could they get the little girl away from him? Legally, they had few rights until Courtney could prove she was Lark's biological mother, and even then, Lowell would most likely try to discredit her character. He'd probably already let the people around them know she'd been taking drugs after giving birth. Without giving the helpful detail that he'd been the one to give them to her. Plus, Sean and Courtney were in a different country's jurisdiction.

Thankfully, Paisley had a volunteer legal team in her network, as well, who worked pro bono for such cases. He'd contact one of them.

Then there was the question of whether the little girl with Lowell was really Lark.

Soon they were on the boat, though it had taken Courtney some maneuvering to board on crutches, and he'd barely resisted the urge to pick her up and carry her. Now, she gripped the metal railing and stared at the ocean, refusing to sit.

When they took off from the dock, Tamara started a motor rather than hoisting the sails, so it seemed a good time to ask. He raised his voice over the motor's noise. "We might need DNA evidence from the little girl."

Tamara cut him a glance as she steered through sloppy waves. "I imagine you'd need to obtain it in secret?"

He cleared his throat and, his chest twinging, resisted the urge to look away. All his life, he'd done everything out in the open. But as they said, desperate times called for desperate measures. "Yes."

"If possible." Courtney twisted her grip on the railing, her fingers pinching white.

"Hmm." Tamara stood stiff behind the wheel. "According to my friend, Lowell and the little girl frequent a little oceanfront café for dinner."

"Yes!" Courtney pumped her fist in the air. "Maybe we can get her cup or napkin after she eats."

While she still retreated into her secluded shell sometimes, she was becoming more assertive, and he welcomed the change. Though a part of him wished it was about something other than stealing a used napkin. He shouldn't judge, though, especially considering he might be the one stealing it.

He shifted his feet. "I'll do it. Lowell could recognize you."

She stared at him, then nodded. "I could wear a disguise, but yes, that makes sense." Then she turned to Tamara. "Are there hotels on the island?"

"Yes, but I already booked you a bungalow for privacy." Tamara grinned over her shoulder.

Courtney's eyes widened. "That's... awesome. Thank you so much."

"Don't mention it." Tamara waved off the gratitude.

He understood better and better why Paisley was so successful. He'd once blurted out, "So what you do is all about computers?"

Paisley had said then, "No, it's all about people. It's all about finding the right people."

And the moment he'd seen Courtney, he knew she was the right person for him. He just knew. As if God had created her specifically for him.

His heart squeezed painfully while ocean spray dampened his face. Would Courtney ever feel the same about him?

Her face was healing, and he prayed and hoped she'd heal enough one day to be open to new possibilities. To be open to a relationship. To be open to a relationship *with him*. He might be inexperienced in romance, but he couldn't be mistaken about her attraction to him. And she wouldn't have kissed him if she didn't feel something for him. Even if she'd said the kiss shouldn't have happened. Just the memory of it fired up his blood.

Responding to it hadn't been a mistake. *She* wasn't a mistake. Whatever the outcome, she was the best thing that had ever happened to him. He couldn't control what he felt for her, and he didn't want to.

Then a thought struck him, and he staggered from it rather than the waves rocking the boat. He gripped the cold, unforgiving railing to steady himself.

What if Lowell gave Courtney an ultimatum: return to him and have her daughter back? Or never see Lark again? What would Courtney choose to do?

Staying with the abusive man who'd manipulated and physically assaulted her was beyond dangerous. But she wouldn't think about herself. She'd sacrifice herself for her daughter. Even though Sean hadn't known her long, he knew enough to guess this.

His gut twisted. He could lose her and lose her soon.

Soon, they could see the lush island coastline. But as much as the greenery and aquamarine waters pleased the eye, he missed the Show Me state and the ranch already. And of course, his family and Ada who was part of his family, really. He missed home. Nostalgia unraveled inside.

His gaze slipped to Courtney, her white T-shirt flapping the wind, her features defiant. She'd taken off her cap, and her dark hair spread over her shoulders, lifted by the wind, like bird wings. Her mouth set in a determined line, the cut on her lip still visible. Her willingness to put herself in harm's way for her daughter when she hadn't even healed yet stirred him.

No, *home* would be wherever Courtney decided to go if she accepted him.

"I'll drop you both off at your bungalow." Tamara spoke loudly. "Then, this evening, I'll pick up Sean and take him to the café Lowell frequents."

"Thank you very much. How about you pick up both of us?" Courtney lifted her hands as if pleading. "Hear me out, please. It's not just because I want to see my daughter as soon as possible. Though... though there's that. But you'd need me to identify Lowell, right?"

"We have his photo," Sean said.

That she'd kept, despite everything, and it grated at Sean. It was their wedding photo, and Courtney looked gorgeous and smitten with her bridegroom.

"Well, but... but we need to make sure." She gripped the railing again and stared at the shore intently as if hoping to see Lark there already. "I can wear a disguise. Paisley gave me a wig in case I needed to hide from Lowell later. I–I'm good with makeup. Got lots of practice. And... there's so much sunshine, so it's only natural to wear sunglasses, right?" She pointed to her aviator sunglasses.

"Right." He didn't want her anywhere near that guy, but he didn't have the heart to say no.

Tamara waved in the air. "It's up to you."

"Thank you so much." Courtney's eyes lit up, and the wind whipped wisps of hair around her face.

He reached to her and tucked it behind her ear. His fingers brushed her smooth skin, giving his heart a stutter. "But you'll have to be careful, okay? You can't, um, run to Lark. You'll have to control your feelings when you see her." If that was Lark. But he didn't add that comment, for Courtney's sake.

Her eyes narrowed. "I will. I have lots of experience controlling my feelings."

While that tweaked his compassion, it also made him frown. Did it mean she'd never let herself fall in love again?

Minutes later, they were inside the bungalow where he brought their luggage from the sailboat. Courtney only had one small suitcase, and his was a duffel bag with clothes hastily thrown together. He placed them on the wooden floor for now, skeptical they'd have everything they needed. He didn't want Courtney to go without.

As if understanding they might need some things they didn't pack, Tamara said, "There's food in the refrigerator and snacks, plus canned food in the cabinets. The bathrooms are well stocked with towels, bathrobes, and toiletries. But if you need some things, there's a convenience store within walking distance. It has summer clothes and footwear, as well."

"Thank you. This is much better than I could've expected." Courtney smiled her gratitude as she moved on her crutches.

The bungalow, decorated with bamboo rugs, woven furniture, azure seascapes, and funky coconut bowls with mangoes and papayas, was elevated over the water and offered two bedrooms and a living room area. Magenta tropical flowers in wooden vases added a vibrant touch and a strong scent. A cushioned footrest crouched on bowed legs as if tired from all the feet that rested there. Sean was thankful for its presence so Courtney could put up her casted foot.

Probably the best thing about the place was a spacious deck with its glass-topped rattan table and matching cushioned chairs and a hammock lounging between two posts that overlooked the spectacular ocean.

This place would be perfect for a honeymoon.

The thought made him wince. He wasn't even dating Courtney, and here he thought about marrying her.

Tamara placed two phones on the bamboo kitchen bar. "These are burner phones. They already have my phone number and my friend's number. Feel free to call anytime. I'll explain the security system, but it's still better to stay under the radar."

Or at the lodge with its state-of-the-art security system. Thankfully, he didn't blurt that out, though based on Courtney's guilty look she had the same thought.

After giving instructions about the security system, Tamara left.

Sean and Courtney were alone. In a romantic tropical paradise. Awareness flushed over him like a crystalline ocean wave. He shifted from one foot to the other. "Um, I don't think they have a pink or yellow room, but you're welcome to choose from whatever rooms they do have here."

She chuckled, the sound reverberating through him. Then she wobbled on crutches toward the first bedroom. "I do miss the yellow room."

When all this was over, was there a chance she'd miss *him*? What a bittersweet thought.

Lord, when the time comes, please help me make the right choice. I want Courtney to be happy. I want her to get her little girl back. But I don't want to lose her. If that's selfish of me, I'm sorry.

He picked up her bag and followed her.

"This room is good for me." She turned around. "How about meeting on the deck after we get settled?"

His chest swelled at the prospect of time alone with her. "I'd love to. I mean, if you're not jetlagged."

"I'm not... unless... unless you are."

With her gaze so uncertain, he cringed. He really knew how to put his foot in his mouth, didn't he? "Totally not. Not at all. Not in the least."

Her lips curved up slightly. "I get the idea."

"Right."

His settling in didn't take much time at all. He unpacked the few things he had, which included two T-shirts, shorts, mismatched socks, and flip-flops of different colors. For some reason, he'd packed Ada's toy, and it squeaked, making his heart squeeze. Cormac had promised to take care of her in Sean's absence, but he still wished his pet was here. As much for the company as to defend Courtney.

Then he returned to the living room and checked the surroundings to ensure nothing outside looked suspicious. Not seeing a single boat, he took a lungful of air and let his gaze drift to the line where the ocean met the sky. Maybe it would be safe enough for Courtney to stay here for some time.

He filled an empty coconut bowl with snacks from the cabinet, then washed, peeled, and cut fruit, and placed the cubes on a mosaic platter. He took that and the snack bowl to the deck. Then he poured mango juice and filled water glasses and carried those on a tray to the rattan table, as well. A beckoning breeze and the faraway screeches of seagulls greeted him. It would be so peaceful if the reason for them being here didn't make his stomach clench.

The click-clack of the crutches announced Courtney's appearance. His eyes widened as she clattered onto the deck. She always managed to take his breath away, be it in a turtleneck and black pants or bundled in a blue parka. But now she affected him even more.

Her dark hair hugged her shoulders now, shadowed by a wide-brimmed white hat. Its scarlet ribbon matched the long dress flowing to her ankles. A scattered pattern of giant red poppies shimmied on her hem as the breeze played with both it and the milky-silky scarf wrapped around her slender neck. Makeup hid her yellowish bruises. Her belt was scarlet, as well, and so were her lips, which gave no evidence that not so long ago they'd been split. Even if he didn't see all the hurt done to her, he still knew about it, and it sent anger coursing through his veins.

Then his gaze stayed on her lips for longer than it should have.

The memory of kissing her made blood rush in his veins. "You look—what is the word?—breathtaking." He pulled out the cushioned chair for her.

"Thank you." She sat gracefully, and he rested the crutches against the house wall, painted turquoise as if to match the ocean. "I've never worn this dress, though I've had it for some time. I–I didn't want to attract attention. I was *scared* of attracting attention."

In his mind, he screamed a few unkind things about Lowell for causing all this damage to her. Then Sean pushed the fruit platter toward her. "It's just you and me now." Though probably not for long. "And you always had my attention."

She looked down and munched on mango cubes. Finally, she said, "As you had mine. You know what? I'm going to wear this dress in public, too. I want Lark back. And I also want myself back."

He leaned forward. "I'll do everything to help you in that."

She sipped her mango juice. "You have no idea how much that means to me. Or that you're helping me stand tall after so many years of standing small."

He brought his glass to his lips and drank some of the sweet liquid, but his gaze never wavered from her. "You'll stand tall. You already are. And soon enough, you'll fly high again."

Probably away from him. He flushed the bitter thought with a saccharine drink.

She stared at the ocean, then at him, her gaze attentive and interested. "I always make it about me. But I want to hear more about you."

"There's not much to say. You know about the ranch and my family already." But maybe she needed to take her mind off seeing the man who'd hurt her so much and the daughter she might never have back. Surely, even he could come up with a few stories to distract her.

"Okay, I can tell you about some things on the ranch." He helped himself to some papaya chunks to fortify his brain and spoke about the farm animals. He even made her crack a smile, which was a huge reward.

Then she said, "If it's okay to ask, why are you still single?"

He placed his empty glass on the table, condensation dripping down its side as if crying silent tears, and leaned back against his rattan chair. The fingers he laced in his lap shook. "I–I fell in love once. Fell hard. We dated for three years. I started planning our lives together in my mind. Bought a ring. Proposed." For a moment, his stomach clenched. He'd pushed those memories away for a long time. "She said no."

"I'm sorry," Courtney whispered.

"She said she wasn't ready for marriage yet. And ranch life wasn't for her, anyway. She didn't think we would've worked out long-term."

It still hurt, but it was an echo of the pain instead of the sharp pain it used to be. It was as if time sanded off the hard edges like the ocean would smooth glass bottle shards. Or maybe it wasn't just time. It was meeting Courtney. "We broke up. Half a year later, I heard she'd married some rich guy in a big city."

Courtney's blue eyes softened and glowed. "It's her loss."

"It didn't feel like that at the time. I was heartbroken. A year after her wedding, I met her by accident when she came to Cowboy Crossing to visit her parents. Since we don't have many restaurants in our small town, she was there with her parents when I went with my brothers. She drove a flashy car, wore flashy diamonds, and sported a flashy smile. She stopped me and told me how much she enjoyed her life now and that she'd never have to work again."

Courtney grimaced but didn't say a word.

He peered at the endless ocean. For the first time since the breakup, he had a calmness and clarity about it as if he'd dived headlong into the ocean attracted by a sparkly treasure, lost it, and now found out the treasure was fake. "Now when I look back, I see it all in a different light. She was right. We wouldn't have worked out long-term. She wasn't the right person for me, and I wasn't the right person for her. It was better for us to have broken up then, rather than to have spent many years together in misery."

"You have an amazing outlook." Those admiring tones made him look again at her.

"Believe me, I didn't always." It was probably not heroic to admit it, but... "I snapped at people after she broke up with me. Then Dad took me on a walk after the rain. I didn't want to go tramp in the mud, but I went. He told me that sometimes we don't like the rain. We'd rather it be sunshine all the time. But rain helps plants and trees grow." He gestured to the ocean. "We need water."

"We do." She reached for her water glass and saluted him with it.

Unlike other people, he didn't know how to explain things well, hence his grouchiness sometimes. But Courtney always seemed to understand him, anyway. "And sometimes we don't like cold and snow. But snow preserves the crops and then becomes water in spring. It was a long walk for me, but it was also the beginning of healing from the breakup."

She trailed a finger over the rim of her water glass. "So what you want to say is...?"

His throat became parched, and he drained his glass. "Something we don't like might become something to help us stay alive later." He clattered his glass back to the table as a thought struck him. "That's not to say I'm trying to justify what happened to you. I just hope something good can come out of it."

"Like Lark." Her eyes softened further, their blues becoming misty.

"Like Lark."

But would she be able to see her little girl without suffering again in the process?

Chapter Fourteen

In the evening, Courtney clasped her hands to stop them from trembling as she sat on the restaurant terrace overlooking the ocean. She and Sean had deliberately arrived early and chosen the least crowded section.

"What would you like to drink?" A lanky young waiter with sandy-blond hair cut in a fade spoke in English as he handed them laminated menus.

"Lemonade." She did her best to change her voice as she answered, and it came out raspy, foreign to her. But at least it didn't tremble like her hands still did.

"Iced tea with lemon for me, please." Worry flashed in Sean's eyes.

"Certainly. Coming right up." The waiter left.

Even though she'd looked the place over before entering the oceanfront terrace, she visually searched it again. Her heart beating way too fast for her liking, she leaned closer to Sean and whispered, "There's no sign of them yet."

On the one hand, it should be reassuring. On the other hand, it made her heart squeeze painfully. What if Lowell and Lark didn't show up at all? She needed to see her songbird, at least to know Lark was alive.

Drawing a deep breath of salty air mixed with scents of fried meat coming from the tables, she faced the cerulean ocean. Its serene waters didn't assuage her turmoil. She nearly jumped in her chair when one of the patrons dropped their keys on the floor.

Had she made a mistake coming here? She turned to Sean, her anchor in the coming storm. "What if he recognizes me, after all?"

Sean stroked her clasped hands with his fingertips, sending her heart racing for a reason other than fear. "He won't. He doesn't expect you here. And you look different. Good different." He cleared his throat. "Stunning." The tips of his ears pinked. "Not that you usually don't look stunning."

A nervous chuckle escaped her lips. "I understood. And... thank you." Some of the tension seemed to dissolve in her veins like salt in ocean waters, and her nerves settled a bit. He had that effect on her.

Lowell had been as smooth as this table surface with words, but Sean's awkwardness endeared him to her. This time, she had to clasp her hands to stop herself from taking his hand, from stroking his face. Her breathing went shallow again. Then something needled. She couldn't allow her feelings to distract her from her mission.

What kind of mother was she?

One without a child.

The waiter brought their drinks then, and Courtney hadn't even looked at the menu. She opened it and pointed at the first thing that caught her eye. "*Fungee* and *pepperpot*." Whatever it was, she was too jittery to eat, anyway.

"Great choice," the guy said in a tone that suggested everyone in this restaurant made a great choice, according to him. Then he turned to Sean. "And for you, sir?"

"I'll try the same." Sean handed over the menu without opening it.

"Very well." The waiter took the menus and disappeared again.

She unclamped her hands and tapped the table. "Do you know what we so carefully chose?"

"I looked at local cuisine on the internet. Fungee is a cornmeal dish made with okra. Pepperpot is a hearty stew."

"Ooooh. Not bad. Could be snails or something." Paying attention to the tables around them, she sipped her tangy drink. Ice cubes clanked in her glass. "Though I'm sure pepperpot can't compare to your mom's stew." She missed it already. She missed his family, and she wasn't even a part of it. Did she want to be?

Yes, but she didn't have the right to try on a new family just because she'd pushed away her own. Her fingers tightened around the cold smooth glass, like Lowell's fingers had tightened around her neck before, cutting off her air supply. She even gulped for air like in those times, then tugged on her silk scarf. This was much cheaper than the fancy one he'd bought her so she could cover the bruises on her neck. Instead of leaving the man, she'd worn that ridiculously expensive scarf like a noose tightening around her neck. Later, she'd bought a bunch of turtlenecks for the times it would be too cold to wear a silk scarf.

"I agree with you. Mom's cooking is amazing. But let's give the pepperpot a chance." His eyes searched hers as if asking her to give *him* a chance as well, to give a chance to whatever was brewing between them while the pepperpot was simmering in the restaurant kitchen.

But she didn't know if she could yet, because her life was going to be uncertain and revolving around Lark. So Courtney looked away and eyed the new arrivals on the terrace.

Then her heart jumped. "Don't look yet, but they just arrived. The dark-haired guy in latte-hued slacks and a white polo shirt. The little girl in pink overalls with an embroidered pony." Her breath caught in her throat. "Her hair... her hair is in pigtails and the same shade as mine."

In that moment, Courtney didn't care about any DNA tests. This was her daughter. Her heart thumped in her ears. Using all her willpower, she pushed herself deeper into her seat, keeping herself from running—okay, hobbling on the crutches—toward the little girl, scooping her daughter in her arms, and never letting go.

She inhaled a deep breath of salty air, then another one for good measure, and reminded herself this was also a little girl who didn't know about her mommy's existence. And might never know.

Her stomach clenched as she lowered her head to make sure the wide-brimmed hat hid her face from Lowell should he look in her direction. Good thing she'd donned aviator sunglasses and the long blonde wig. She'd never worn red lipstick before, and she'd applied it beyond the contour of her lips to make them appear larger. She'd added an artificial birthmark in the corner of her mouth and another on her cheek. She'd barely recognized herself in the mirror, but what if *he* still recognized her?

The young waiter set a tray in front of her, and she nearly screamed at him to step aside and not block the view. Her heart thumped harder, more terrified of Lark disappearing like a mirage than she was terrified of Lowell.

Sean touched her hand as if to say everything was going to be all right. Then he nodded to the waiter. "Thank you."

She just managed a few nods.

"Let me know if you need anything else." With those words, the man walked away.

And she exhaled her pent-up breath. Lark was still there. Courtney scoured the precious child for signs of abuse, but like Tamara had said, none were visible. The girl laughed at something. The sound was music to Courtney's ears, and her thudding heartbeat settled into a survivable rhythm. Then it started galloping again.

What if her disguise wasn't good enough and Lowell recognized her?

She shuddered. Not only because her body remembered all too well the damage the man now sitting a few feet away had inflicted but also because she could ruin everything.

Hadn't he often said she *always* ruined everything?

Sean squeezed her hand, giving her much-needed strength. "He won't hurt you anymore. Ever. I promise."

As the ocean basked in the sun's golden glow, she basked in his luminous brown eyes and found her personal sunshine aglow in their depths.

Something inside her shifted and changed forever. He was the sunshine that thawed her dormant heart after a very, very, *veeeeery* long winter. Only she couldn't tell him that yet. She could barely admit it to herself.

He said grace, and then she took a spoonful of flavorful soup as if it were bitter medicine and pushed it around the lump in her throat. Dipping her head, she straightened unsubstantial wrinkles on her silk dress. She'd paired the poppy dress with a bright jacket, going with the idea of hiding in plain sight and choosing bright colors for her outfit and makeup.

Nearly all her life she'd dressed in grayish or dark colors. She'd done her best to stay unnoticed. While growing up, she'd learned fast that, if she'd stayed unnoticed, maybe she wouldn't get yelled at, wouldn't get hit. Same thing in school to avoid bullying. A girl from a poor family dressed in her sister's hand-me-downs had been an easy target. She'd even dreamed of being invisible.

Some animals learned to hide to survive. They'd had to. Insects that managed to blend into the background wouldn't get eaten by birds.

Only she wasn't an insect. She glanced again at the ocean to remind herself how far she'd come from that cowering person, and not just in a geographic sense. Besides the spray jasmine-scent mist, her apple-red knit hat and mittens had been some of the first things she'd bought after her divorce.

Now more than her hopes to hide in plain sight prompted her to choose her disguise. Lowell would never expect her to look like this.

She lifted her chin as she scooped a spoonful of hearty pepperpot. She didn't just look different. She *was* a different person, and a lot of it was thanks to Sean. She needed that strength. Lark deserved a mother who could protect her, something Courtney's own had never been able to do. Courtney's heart constricted.

Watching the little girl, Courtney sipped the cool sweet liquid of her lemonade. It was time to polish that newly found spine to a shine rivaling the silverware where it caught the setting sun's light.

"It's her," she whispered to Sean. Or did she want it to be? She'd painted so many pretty pictures in her head in her lifetime of the things she'd wanted so desperately.

A caring father.

A loving husband.

A happy house.

Was she now painting the picture of a lost-and-found daughter?

"We'll still do what we decided to make sure," she added fast.

Which meant they'd have to linger at their table until Lowell and Lark left. That wouldn't be a hardship. She could look into Sean's brown eyes and get lost there forever. Or at least, far longer than it would take to eat dinner.

"But what happens after we get the results?" She voiced what she and Sean must both be thinking.

Sean rubbed his jaw. "We'll have to find some way to persuade Lowell to give up parental rights."

"But how? And what if she's happy with him? What if she doesn't need me? I'd never want to harm her in any way."

His gaze caressed her. "I'll help you in whatever you decide."

"I don't deserve you." She breathed out as she finished her pepperpot much faster than she'd expected. And here she'd thought she wouldn't be able to eat a single bite.

"You do. And you deserve to be happy."

The words touched her to the core. "Thank you. You, too." Which also meant he deserved much better than what her life was.

The lanky waiter showed up again. "Would you like anything else?"

They'd need to order dessert if they were going to stay here a while, so she nodded. "What do you have for desserts?"

The waiter brightened as if she'd just given him a birthday present. "May I recommend *ducana*? It's a dumpling made from sweet potatoes, grated coconut, spices, sugar, and flour. It's cooked in banana leaves in boiling water."

"Kind of like tamales?" she asked.

"I presume."

She smiled. "Sounds good to me."

As the waiter walked away, Sean's words echoed in her mind, then took hold. She wanted to be happy, but the two people who meant so much to her—Sean and Lark—couldn't be wrapped together with a pretty bow like a Christmas present. Chances were, she'd have to let him go. Her heart ached at the thought.

She drained her lemonade as emotions parched her throat and a simple truth set her blood on fire.

She'd never meant to fall in love again. But she'd fallen for Sean. She had no doubt about it now as if the words were written in the sky and impossible to ignore.

Then Lark's chirpy-sweet voice reached her. "Daddy, Daddy, can I go swimming tomorrow?"

Courtney didn't hear what Lowell replied. She didn't have any doubts about something else too. She knew her former husband well. He'd use their daughter as leverage. He'd tell Courtney that, if she ever wanted to see Lark again, they'd have to become one happy family.

And as she gazed at this incredible man supporting her, she knew she loved him. But she'd never, ever give up on her daughter.

Chapter Fifteen

Despite his worries for Courtney and the future, Sean resolved to make the best of the days with a wonderful woman in a wonderful place.

Today marked their fourth day since they'd obtained the DNA sample and mailed in the kit. He poured orange juice and added a few ice cubes to the glasses, then took them outside to the deck.

Courtney relaxed in the hammock, crutches on the wood planks nearby. But at the sight of him, she sat, and her lips curved up. "You didn't have to bring me a drink. But I sure appreciate it."

And he appreciated every minute spent in her company. Especially considering those minutes could soon slip away like water through his fingers. Every day and every minute, he'd been falling more and more for her.

He didn't dare to say it, though, so he just shrugged. "No problem."

"Stay with me for a while, please." She peered over the rim before taking a slow sip from her glass.

He'd stay forever and ever with her—if she'd let him.

Her gaze and request unfurled heat in his belly, but she needed his emotional support, something she'd sadly never gotten from other people. She already carried a lot on her shoulders and didn't need the additional burden of him talking about his feelings.

"Sure," he said, grouchier than he'd intended.

He could've brought a chair, but he opted to sit on the wooden planks, warmed by the sun, legs dangling over the edge of the deck.

For precious moments, they peered at the sparkling ocean and listened to its whisper. Too bad they couldn't stroll along the beach, but it wouldn't be easy while her crutches sank into the sand.

Unless he carried her...

Warmth nearly melted him again, and it had nothing to do with the sun shining on them. He'd never been much of a talker, and right now, he didn't need to be. Silence with her had never been awkward but comforting. Just being in her presence, he basked in a pleasant feeling.

He could spend a lifetime like that. He could spend a lifetime with her.

Even if he missed the ranch, Ada, and his family.

She seemed to read his mind. "This place is gorgeous. But I miss Ada. And the lodge. And your family. I hope you won't have to miss Christmas with them because of me."

"Things can still change before Christmas." He took in her butterscotch-hued blouse—the color of sunshine, she'd called it—the magenta tropical flower tucked behind her ear, and the newfound confidence in her eyes. She'd been changing, and he liked those changes.

She swirled her glass, frowning at it as the ice cubes clinked, and her eyes became pensive. "Waiting for the DNA results is torture. But even more is not knowing what I'll do after we do receive the results."

"Okay, let's see what we know so far thanks to Paisley and my cop brother." He did his best to put on a problem-solver hat, but it wasn't as easy as donning a cowboy hat. "Before coming here for a month, Lowell hadn't moved to Europe like he'd told you. He'd taken a well-paid position in Seattle. Paisley created a fake but beautiful magazine about prominent businessmen in the city. All so Madeline could pose as its reporter and write a human-interest story about Lowell. Madeline talked to his colleagues and neighbors about what kind of father he is, as well as his career accomplishments." The results surprised Sean.

"Yes, and they all said that he was a good father, though he did work a lot." Courtney's eyes narrowed. "The longtime nanny refused to give an interview. She probably signed a nondisclosure agreement."

Gathering information was risky, considering word could get back to Lowell. Or was Courtney silently saying goodbye to her daughter?

The unfairness of it all struck Sean like a tsunami. Courtney had suffered so much and had gone through much.

Lord, doesn't she deserve to be with her child?

With all his heart, Sean wanted to help her, and he didn't know how. But he knew people who possibly did. "His colleagues said he took a well-deserved vacation to spend more time with his daughter. But nobody knew where exactly."

"So I guess after his detour to beat me up, he went on that well-deserved vacation." Courtney's voice soured, and the glass in her hand shook, making ice cubes clank again.

His heart went out to her, and he placed his hands atop hers to steady the glass. But what would steady his rapid pulse? "We'll find a way to bring him to justice for what he did. And I'm wondering if he did the same thing to other women. Not... not that I'd want him to. It's just that people usually don't change."

"I agree. Maybe we can launch some investigation with Ronan and Paisley's help?"

"I'm sure they'll be on board. And Madeline knows a fantastic local private investigator who did an amazing job with Madeline's personal case." Once her hands stopped shaking, he reluctantly let them go.

"You have an amazing family, but then, I said that already. If there are more women Lowell abused, I want to help them. And okay, that would help my case, too. His lawyer is very skillful, so if I went to court, he'd find ways to prove I'd be an unfit mother. But I wouldn't want Lark to get hurt. And she'd be hurt if I exposed the truth about him." She drained her juice and thudded the empty glass onto the deck.

She always thought of others. It was one of many things he admired about her. Her lips, so close to his, beckoned, reminding him of the euphoria when she'd kissed him on the plane. He looked away to stop himself from leaning toward her.

"What if... what if he senses something and leaves the island with Lark? I could lose track of her."

He did his best to channel his wayward thoughts toward matters at hand. "Ronan and Jessie have been trailing him since they arrived yesterday. That's also to make sure Lark is safe with him. Tamara said there have been no strange incidents since he and the girl arrived on the island. Did you receive any more emails from him?"

"Yes." Her eyes darkened, and her lips set in a tight line. "I've been sending my answers to Paisley first, and she's sent the responses to appear to have come from Missouri. He—he's been saying how much he misses me. That he loves me still. That things could be different."

"What a jerk!" Sean ground his teeth.

"I answered him with questions about Lark and asked for more photos. Not because I believed his usual tricks, but because I didn't want him to get suspicious. And yes, because I wanted to know more about my daughter. He hasn't answered any questions but sent more photos." Her lower lip trembled.

"All these years missed... All the time I could've held her in my arms. Wiped her tears. Soothed her."

She kept quiet for some time. Then she lifted her chin again. "Tamara also said he's been meeting with a woman regularly on the island. One of the vacationers."

Was Courtney jealous? The thought sliced Sean. "Do you... do you still have feelings for him? I mean not that it's any of my business."

"Yes." She stared somewhere past him. Into her past?

"Right." He suppressed a frown. "It's none of my business."

"It's not that. I meant, yes, I do have feelings for him." She didn't even think before answering.

"Oh." His heart sank onto the deck.

"Those feelings are contempt and some fear," she said every word as if she spat it out.

"Oh," he said again, but this time his heart returned to its dutiful place in his chest.

What feelings did she have toward him, Sean? Although desperate to know, he didn't have the right to ask when she was in such a difficult situation.

The ocean breeze whipped her long hair across her face, and he got up and eased it aside. He did it for himself more than for her. He craved to see her face, her eyes. But the gesture might've been a mistake because his fingers brushed her smooth skin, and his pulse skyrocketed. Apparently, even a simple touch wreaked havoc on his senses.

Her eyes widened, and her breathing went shallow as if she felt something, too. As if she felt a lot. Longing appeared in her eyes. Before he could stop himself, he leaned to her, his heartbeat a staccato now. He needed to kiss her more than he needed his next breath.

Then the phone rang in his pocket, nearly making him gnash his teeth at the untimely interruption.

Apprehension replaced the longing in her eyes. "You might want to get that. Could be Ronan."

Doing his best to ignore his disappointment, he fished out the phone. "You're right." He swiped the screen to answer his cop brother's call.

"We got the DNA results." Ronan didn't waste time on pleasantries. "Feel free to put me on speakerphone if Courtney is there with you."

"She is." Sean put his brother on speakerphone, then frowned as he looked at Courtney. She'd authorized Paisley and several other members of his family to have access to the DNA results, but he didn't expect them so fast.

"The test resulted in"—Ronan paused for a sharp breath—"a match. Courtney, you're this child's mother."

She must've expected it, but her eyes went huge.

Too many emotions struggled inside Sean. While thrilled for her to have found the child she'd grieved for so long, he suspected Lowell wouldn't just agree to joint custody or visitation rights. Lowell wanted Courtney back. Diminishing her made him feel better about himself.

Sean's teeth gnashed for a different reason. He'd never want her to suffer.

Lowell's taunting emails made Sean fear that, to have her daughter back, she'd put herself at risk and return to her ex. Would he lose her forever?

"I don't have any other choice. I *have* to go and talk to him." Courtney covered her face as she sat on a woven living room chair in the oceanfront bungalow.

No. Enough.

She'd been hiding behind her fingers, like a child, for way too long. It had to stop, and it had to stop now. She let her hands drop and raised her chin to Sean.

He paced the bamboo rug, stumbled over the footrest, told the innocent footrest some unflattering words, and resumed pacing.

She moved the footrest closer to her, stroked its smooth fabric surface as if to comfort it, and placed her cast-clad foot on it. It wasn't easy to defy the man she loved—even if he might never know about her love. Besides, her default response was to recoil, placate, and hide.

Even though Sean wasn't a threat but trying to protect her from one.

"Please try to understand. Paisley reported that Lowell just resigned from the company in Seattle. He can whisk Lark anywhere in the world. And next time, I might not be able to find her. I..." Her heart twisted, and she took a deep breath tinged with the tang of tropical fruits. "I know Paisley should be able to find his IP address, but what if he stops writing to me? I can't risk it."

"But what if he turns violent again?" Sean forked his fingers through his hair, yanking at it as he stopped pacing and stood in front of her. His gaze moved to her cast, then to the crutches stacked near the chair.

He didn't say anything further, and she didn't need him to. Unlike now, the previous time she could physically run from Lowell, and it still had ended tragically. Would've ended worse if Sean hadn't found her. She shivered at the memory of fists and boots coming toward her. Not just one memory. Many of them. The sight of the Christmas ornament crushed under his boot before he slammed that boot into her face.

Now Sean crouched beside her chair and brushed the back of his hand against her cheek, sending a delicious wave through her despite her turmoil. "I want you to get your daughter back. I do. But I want you to be safe, too."

"That's why you can be somewhere nearby when I go see him." She pulled her shoulders back. "As well as Ronan and Jessie. We can ask them to provide backup. I–I can't hide from Lowell forever. Besides, it's better to have an element of surprise than have him find me alone someday."

His Adam's apple bobbed as he swallowed hard. "I'm... still not comfortable with that plan. But I don't have a better one."

As Sean's proximity unnerved and comforted her, she hugged her arms around herself, part of her wishing they were *his* arms—no, right now, she needed to stand on her own. Or, well, sit on her own. "He'll expect me to cower in front of him again. But he doesn't expect the new me. Besides, it's not like he's going to *shoot* me. If he starts hitting me, you'll show up, right?"

"And if I don't agree, you'll sneak out in the middle of the night, right?" His eyes darkened as if he regretted his words.

Ouch.

She winced. She deserved that reminder.

"Okay, I shouldn't have said that." His eyes dimmed.

"I don't want to. I have the right to see my daughter." This was the first time she'd talked about her rights. Her entire life seemed to consist of obligations, first to be a good daughter and sister, then to be a good wife. "So please agree."

"What if he locks the door?"

"I'll find a way to unlock it." Her gaze moved to the seascape depicting a storm. A similar storm was pummeling her soul. But she wasn't just trying to hold on to whatever was left after the shipwreck to keep afloat. She was trying to save something important and dear to her. "Lowell didn't answer my last two emails. Maybe he suspects something. Here's something else. I can try to record him admitting that he deceived me and kidnapped Lark."

"I doubt it would hold up in court." His tone softened the strike of the words.

Frowning, she raked her fingers through her hair. He was right. Of course, he was right. But she couldn't turn around and leave the island when the daughter she'd long considered lost to her was alive and so very close. Her heart ached for her little girl.

And she also couldn't walk away from Lark because how could she be sure Lowell would never hurt his daughter? Eventually, he'd need a new punching bag, and just the thought iced Courtney's veins, despite the warm air. She looked at the tropical flowers now withering in a vase. She'd let Lowell cut her off from her family, from her roots, but she wasn't just going to wither away. And she wouldn't let him cut her off from her daughter, too.

Sean's phone beeped with a text, and he ignored it. Then he reached into his pocket. "Might be Ronan, right?"

"Of course. Please answer." She nodded and tensed. If Sean's cop brother contacted him, he might have some news. Or Lowell might be on the move.

Sean checked the text message, then looked up at her. "Lowell and Lark just left their bungalow in a taxi." His eyes narrowed. "They were leaving with bags."

"What?" She jumped to her feet—er, well, to one foot.

"Maybe they're going to just spend some time on the larger island." But his voice said he didn't believe this excuse.

Frantically, she searched the ferry schedule on her phone, then nearly dropped it. "Even if we pack fast, we won't make it to the ferry in time."

"I'll call Tamara."

Without bothering with crutches, she hopped into her room and threw her clothes in the suitcase. She could compete in speed with a bunny running from a wolf. She didn't care to pick up toiletries.

Why did she wait for the DNA results? In her heart, she'd known the little girl was her songbird.

Sean met her outside her room. "Ronan texted again. Lowell and Lark are heading toward the ferry. But Tamara is on the way to us."

She ached for her plane, to be able to fly. "He's going to take her somewhere else. He... he must've felt something. Or maybe he wants her to spend Christmas at home." Her stomach twisted. "This is the busiest time of the year. We won't get tickets."

He took her face in his, anchoring her again before she became adrift in the sea of despair. "Paisley can track his IP address when Lowell starts sending emails again. We'll find him and Lark. We won't give up. We'll follow them. Unless they go to the moon. But we'll find a way to follow them even there."

That was right.

She'd never give up.

Chapter Sixteen

Sean's stomach twisted as he carried Courtney into the airport because it was faster than her hobbling there on crutches. If he hadn't asked her to wait for the DNA results, if he hadn't tried to talk her out of confronting Lowell, maybe she could've struck some agreement with the man.

Or not.

Sean's muscles screamed from exertion. Good thing Tamara had promised to ship the things they'd packed and whatever they'd forgotten to the lodge. He shouldn't enjoy having Courtney in his arms, but breathing in her jasmine scent, he cherished these moments close to her.

As soon as he entered the small airport, Ronan and his wife approached, their faces grim.

Reluctantly, Sean put Courtney down.

"Any news?" they asked in unison.

Ronan grimaced. "They are flying to Florida. I overheard Lowell talking to the girl. There's only one flight a day there, and it's completely booked. So are the flights to the nearby states. The next flight to Florida is in two days."

"Sorry, Courtney," Jessie said. "We added all our names to the standby list."

Courtney closed her eyes, then opened them again, determination shining in them. "Maybe something can be done. I'm afraid they'll fly somewhere else out of Florida. And he can try to cover his digital tracks. I can't lose sight of Lark. I need to be on the same plane."

He scooped her up again. "Let's go to the ticket counter." He prayed for a miracle while he carried her there. His prayer had been answered when Paisley had managed to get a first-class ticket for him to the island. But could he hope for two miracles in a row?

The young slim male clerk raised a brow but didn't comment when Sean set Courtney down to stand on one foot. "How may I help you?"

"Have you had any ticket cancellations for the Florida flight?" Sean prayed for a miracle again.

"Please?" Courtney's voice turned pleading.

"I'm sorry, sir, but—"

Breathing fast, a bald man with a belly that threatened to pop the buttons on his Hawaiian shirt rushed to the counter and interrupted the clerk. "I need to return two tickets."

Sean held his breath. When the man said the destination—Chicago via a connecting out of Miami—Sean nearly jumped. "We'll take those Florida tickets, please."

While the clerk performed the transactions, the former passenger wiped sweat from his gleaming head and turned to Sean. His breathing slowed down, thankfully, but a sweat drop traveled down his bulbous nose and dropped to the tile floor. "Can you imagine? My wife had a fight with my mother and decided last minute we're *not* going to return to Florida to spend Christmas with our family." He took a deep breath and sighed. The buttons squirmed but held on for dear life.

The clerk still seemed to make a wise decision to move out of their trajectory.

"I'm sorry, man." Sean did his best to be compassionate while his gratitude was spilling over more than the guy's belly did.

"Sorry?" The guy grinned. "Are you kidding me? I can spend more days sipping drinks in peace at the beach instead of shoveling snow or listening to everyone bickering at the table. *That's the best Christmas ever!*"

Courtney winced and paled at the last sentence, but then she brightened once they had their tickets.

Ronan and Jessie joined them soon. "We'll follow you as soon as we can get tickets on a flight." Then once they were out of the other passengers' earshot, Ronan added, "I overheard something else while Lowell was talking on the phone. He arranged for a local babysitter tomorrow. It looks like he rented an Airbnb out of town and has some kind of meeting."

Worry flashed in Courtney's eyes, but then she pushed her shoulders back. "Hmm. It might be a good time to talk to him. I wouldn't want Lark to overhear us arguing."

Sean ground his teeth. There was *never* a good time to talk to Lowell, but for Courtney's sake, he didn't voice that.

They couldn't let Lowell see them, so Sean and Courtney stayed in a different area waiting for the flight while his brother and his wife went to get some water.

Then Courtney took Sean's hands in hers, sending a jolt to his heart. "Once we know where Lowell and Lark are staying, I'll have to try to make him let me see my daughter. We'll be in the US. You can call the police if he gets angry and uses his fists on me."

"I promised I'd do all I can to help you. And I will. That doesn't mean I have to like you being in possible danger."

"I need to do this. For my daughter. Please." She squeezed his hands, then wrapped her arms around him. Besides that accidental kiss on the plane, she hadn't initiated physical contact with him before.

For a few moments he'd treasure forever, she stayed in his arms, his heart beating fast for many reasons. He'd love to stay like that for a long time.

Then she eased out of his embrace. "Let's figure out what exactly we're going to do tomorrow."

The next day, Courtney thought she could do it, but the moment she saw Lowell opening the door, everything inside her trembled. "Hello, Lowell." How she hated that squeak her voice became.

"Well, well, well. What a surprise." His smile was suave and self-assured. Like so many times before, it sent a shiver down her back.

At first, his eyes had widened when she'd showed up at his rental's doorstep. But now he slipped into his usual role—the confident, successful businessman—with the same ease he slipped into the expensive shirts she'd dutifully starched and ironed for him.

"Come on in." He led her across sparkling latte-hued tiles to a room that apparently served as an office.

Her crutches beat a much slower staccato against that floor than her heart beat against her ribs. Her mind barely registered the brown leather sofas cornering the glass-topped coffee table or the large paintings of red roses. Lowell had always given her red roses, even when he'd known she preferred jasmine. At the time, she'd been beyond thrilled he'd given her any flowers at all. Later, she'd been beyond thrilled when she could go for days without him giving her bruises. That sent another shiver through her.

Those rose paintings boasted gilded frames, like the large photos of her and Lowell he'd put behind glass. He'd put her behind glass, as well. When she'd finally left, she'd thrown those photos on the floor. Childish and silly, and she'd cut her fingers on the shards when she'd tried to pick them up. That was what her marriage to Lowell had been—something broken that had cut her to the core while leaving specks of golden dust.

Fear snatched her spine. She should've waited for Ronan and Jessie to get to Florida for backup. But Courtney had been too afraid Lowell might escape somewhere else.

He waved for her to sit in an armchair and sat behind a massive cherrywood desk. Unlike his usual suits and polished leather shoes, he wore white slacks and a white shirt—a contrast to his raven-black hair, trimmed beard, and mustache—and was barefoot as if he were still on the island. Maybe whoever he expected wasn't coming for a business meeting. "Hmm, I didn't expect you to find me here. Would you like something to drink?"

So you can drug me again?

She kept the words to herself. "No thanks."

"Well, I knew you'd return to me sooner or later. Preferably sooner." Arrogance flashed in his eyes.

She resisted the urge to raise her arms to protect her vital organs. Instead, she raised her chin. "I want to see Lark. And then I want joint custody. It's my right."

He leaned back against his burgundy leather chair. "After you gave up your daughter?"

She recoiled. "I never did!"

He waved dismissively. "You just don't remember or don't want to remember. I guess you couldn't be responsible for your actions. You were taking a lot of drugs at the time. Even the neighbors noticed."

"Drugs you gave me!" She grimaced at how high-pitched her voice sounded, but it was better than a squeak. "After you kidnapped my daughter and gave her to someone else!"

"That's what you say to justify yourself. Anyway, I have a much better suggestion." He smiled again, but the joyless twist of his mustache looked like a scowl. "We can become one happy family. Me, you, and Lark."

Though she'd expected his words, something as hot as lava sluiced through her veins. She ground her teeth and clenched her fists at her sides. "I'll *never* get back with you."

"Then you'll never see Lark again." He got up. "I'll walk you through the door."

"Wait!" Her mind whirled as she raised herself and reached for the crutches.

His smile widened. "Yes?"

"You can't get away with this." She sank onto the chair again.

"Your naïveté is one of the main things I liked about you." He glanced at his watch. "We need to continue this conversation some other time. Somewhere more pleasant. There's an excellent local restaurant where we can meet for the first date of our reconciliation."

The audacity! She nearly choked.

Then it dawned on her. He was expecting someone. Maybe she could use that to her advantage. "I'm fine talking right here. I have DNA results proving Lark is my daughter. How are you going to explain your lie that she's Naomi's daughter who you knew nothing about until Naomi died?"

"Well, you didn't want the child and deceived me by giving Lark to Naomi. I had no clue until you brought up this DNA test. Imagine my devastation and surprise." A lonely tear escaped his eye. "Despite everything, I forgave you. I just love you so very much, Sweet Pea." He leaned toward her across the desk, giving her a whiff of the expensive perfume she'd learned to hate.

Her heart sank. "Do you think people would believe you?"

"I can be persuasive. As can my lawyers. You know that, don't you? But I need to leave now." His smile strained at the corners.

Her gaze traveled to the enlarged framed photos of jellyfish on the wall. Tentacles of sadness and regret tightened around her heart and squeezed. That was what he'd made her into. A jellyfish. Someone spineless.

But not any longer.

A predatory smile lifted his lips. "Don't take too much time to think, though. I might withdraw my generous offer. Take Lark to some country you didn't even know existed."

Rage shot through her. She sprang to her feet—foot—and marched to him. Okay, wobbled toward him on the crutches he'd put her on, which was way less intimidating, but she made up for it with a glare. She hoped.

She resisted the urge to hit him with a crutch because she wouldn't stoop to his level. Anger blinded her as the years of abuse, humiliation, and threats flooded her brain. "Now, listen, you miserable, overinflated excuse for a human being. If you ever think of stealing my daughter away from me again, I'll find you. Even at the bottom of the ocean. At the bottom of the barrel where scum like you should dwell."

He laughed, but it wasn't his usual derisive laugh. A note of uncertainty underplayed it. "Oh please. I'll crush you like a bug. Or a fly, if you prefer."

She ignored his dig at her now being a pilot and his attempt to dismiss her. She straightened her freshly polished spine. "Oh really? I know things you don't want made public, and I'll find every one of your transgressions. I'm not a bug, but *you* will be. One under the public's microscope. I'll fight for Lark whom you kidnapped from me, and I'll fight hard. You have absolutely no idea what I'm capable of." Which was true. She didn't even know herself.

His eyes widened. "What–what got into you? How—Why are you like that?"

Anger pumping her blood fast, she plopped onto the desk, leaned to him, and stared him down. It wasn't a good idea to antagonize him, but she couldn't stop herself. "You know why? Because I'm a survivor. And you're a loser, so weak and insecure you have to beat up a woman to feel better about your worthless, pathetic self."

She could finally breathe with her full chest. Despite two broken ribs. Because her bones were healing, and maybe her soul could, too.

Lowell snatched the front of her blouse into his fist, which mildly irritated her—yes, as if a bug crawled onto her skin—instead of making her terrified like before. "Now listen, Courtney—"

The female shriek behind her made him release her blouse. "I knew it! I knew you were cheating on me! Who is she?"

Uh-oh. Courtney glanced back.

And found herself looking at the barrel of a gun.

Chapter Seventeen

Courtney's heart jumped into her throat. She'd expected danger from Lowell, but not from his unhinged… girlfriend, maybe? It was partly Courtney's fault because she'd unlocked the front door behind herself before following Lowell to the office, but it was for Sean to enter, if needed. Now, she mentally begged him to stay where he was. Even better if he could listen to the conversation on the speakerphone and record it. She couldn't let him catch a bullet.

The pretty newcomer with beach-blonde straight long hair wore blue jeans and a shirt with a cheerful pink flowered pattern, but her expression was anything but cheerful.

Lowell lifted his arms in a placating gesture. "This isn't what you think, Brooke."

"Do you think I'm stupid?" Brooke scowled at him. "You were drawing her close." Her gun moved toward Courtney, causing blood to crystallize in her veins.

The next moment, Sean stormed inside the house. "Ma'am, please put down the weapon."

Worry warred with Courtney's relief.

Brooke blinked, and her mouth slid open. But the gun stayed steady and aimed. "And who are you?"

Sean stepped in front of Courtney, shielding her. "I'm with Courtney."

And she wanted to be with him. Forever. She stepped around him because she couldn't let him take the bullet meant for her.

Right now, when her entire life concentrated on the end of a barrel, she saw with clarity as if a laser cut through her eye retinas. She did want a family of three. She desperately longed for it. But it wasn't with Lowell and Lark. It was with Sean and Lark, which sounded like an impossible dream right now.

The gun shook in Brooke's hands as she scowled at Courtney. "So you're cheating on your man with my man."

Courtney groaned. "Nobody is cheating on anybody!" She recalled some woman Lowell had apparently seen on the island. "Well, if Lowell is cheating, it's *not* with me."

"Courtney, you're not helping!" he shouted.

"I'm not trying to help you." Courtney searched for the right words. She'd better find them because she couldn't even imagine something happening to Sean. She went cold just at the thought.

Meanwhile, Brooke's eyes narrowed. "Lowell, you'd be kissing her if I hadn't shown up."

Despite the situation, Courtney couldn't help scoffing. "Ma'am, please don't shoot. He's not worth it. I mean, I'd be tempted to pummel him with my fists, but he's not worth even that. And trust me, I'll never kiss this man again." Too late, she realized her gaffe.

"Again?" Brooke screeched. She had a rather loud voice. If a fire truck had her, they wouldn't need the siren. Then her face turned the color of said fire truck as she spat at Lowell. "So you kissed her before! I knew it! Did you go to the Caribbean Islands to meet with her? Did you bring her from there?"

"Brooke, please!" Lowell's hands remained hidden. Was he trying to reach a gun hidden somewhere in a drawer? "Why would I be meeting with her here if I knew you were about to show up?"

"You didn't know you'd forget to lock the front door and I'd walk in on you two." Then Brooke moved the gun toward Courtney again. "You're not going to steal my man!"

Courtney's heart dropped onto the sky-blue rug. She needed to correct her mistake and defuse the situation. If only she'd waited for Ronan and Jessie to get here in a few days. Getting shot was undesirable to start with, but getting shot because of Lowell was just adding insult to the injury.

"Believe me, I'm not stealing your man. I wouldn't want Lowell if he was tied with a bow to a luxury car and holding the best cake in the world. I don't even want to be in a hundred-mile vicinity of him. I don't want to breathe the same air as him."

"You made your point, Courtney. You never knew how to say the right thing, did you?" Lowell smirked, then turned to Brooke. "This is all just a misunderstanding."

"Let's all sit down and talk." Sean stepped in front of Courtney again.

Courtney's mind whirled. Could she knock the gun away with her crutch, or was it too risky?

Brooke's eyes narrowed at Courtney. "Well, if you wouldn't even breathe the same air as Lowell, why were you here? Sitting on the table in front of him? Leaning to him?"

Blood thudded in Courtney's head. "Ma'am, Lowell isn't the prize you think he is. He and I are divorced. We have a daughter whom he hid from me. I want to see my daughter again. That's all. That's the only reason I'm here."

Hopefully, that would resolve the issue. Courtney took a shaky breath. It should, right? She peeped from around Sean's massive frame.

"See? It's all in the past, darling." Lowell's voice turned suave as always. He added quickly as if to make sure there was no confusion, "Brooke, darling, you know how much I love you. I didn't mean it at all when I told Courtney that she, our daughter, and I could be one happy family."

Courtney gasped. Not because he'd admitted his words had been a lie—she'd *known* it to be a lie, but because of how Brooke could interpret them.

"So you were going to get back with your ex?" Brooke screeched. "Well, if I can't have you, nobody will!"

Sean threw Courtney on the ground while two shots thundered simultaneously.

Chapter Eighteen

"We should've gotten there sooner."

Sean paced the hospital hall while Ronan hung his head the next day. His gut twisted. While he still didn't have answers to many of his questions about Courtney, the one thing he could do was reassure his brother.

Sean stopped pacing and stared at the cream-colored wall where painted tropical flowers bloomed. The bright crimson and orange flowers failed to lift his mood, maybe because the walls were saturated with the human worries and sufferings that also bloomed in hospitals. "It's not your fault, bro. Seriously. You and Jessie helped Courtney and me tremendously already."

Her hair cut short, Jessie walked toward them in the hall, bringing a tray with paper cups and the scent of coffee, as well as a slight citrus aroma. "Is Courtney still with Lowell in the ICU?" Like the woman herself, the question was matter of fact, but a deep concern settled in her eyes.

"Yes. Thanks for the coffee." Sean took one of the cups. After all, maybe the hot liquid could soften the painful boulder-sized lump in his throat. "I admit I had nothing but disdain for the man. Okay, that came out wrong." He paused and shoved his free hand in his pocket. "I also had contempt for him. But I never imagined anything like this could happen."

"I don't think anyone did, much less Lowell himself." Jessie lifted her cup.

Lowell and Brooke had fired nearly at the same time, but Lowell had missed while Brooke hadn't. As soon as she'd realized she'd shot him, she'd dropped the gun and rushed to him, sobbing. Sean had called the police and requested an ambulance then. Once the police had arrived, they'd arrested Brooke. Sean and Courtney had given their statements.

It all seemed surreal, like something from a movie. Or a book.

The liquid was hot, but Sean took a sip from his anyway. The boulder in his throat didn't move, as if lodged there forever. "How is this going to affect Courtney? Or Lark? That little girl has gone through too many tragedies already." His heart went out to the child, who was now with a social worker while Courtney's custody request was considered. He loved this child he'd never known simply because she was part of Courtney.

They held hands and prayed for Lark, Courtney, and even Lowell.

Then Jessie's lips set into a firm line. "We need to prevent Lark from going into the system while all the legalities are sorted out." Jessie had been in the foster care system and survived by bonding with her foster sisters, but they'd still gone through many hardships. "Paisley and her network are working on it."

Working on it?

Jessie shrugged in response to their silent question. "I've learned many important things with Paisley. One—don't underestimate her. Two—don't question her."

"I know Courtney will do everything to get Lark back. And… and I'd gladly adopt her. I mean, if Courtney agrees to marry me. I mean…" he stumbled. He never knew how to express himself well.

But then, he didn't need to.

"Wow! Bro, congratulations!" Ronan patted him on the back.

Jessie hugged him.

"But if Lark doesn't accept me, that means Courtney won't, either." And while it would break Sean's heart, he wouldn't blame Courtney.

Then the click-clack of crutches on the gray tile hospital floor announced Courtney's arrival. She blinked bloodshot eyes, her face gaunt. "I never—*never*—meant to provoke this."

Everything in Sean came alive at the sight of her. As compassion softened his tense muscles, he placed his cup on an empty plastic seat and met her halfway. Then he told her what he'd told his brother. "It's not your fault. Not your fault at all."

She looked up at him, a tear escaping. "I used to love him so much. Then I learned to hate him. But now, it's just sorrow and sadness. I don't know whether I'll ever fully forgive him for abusing me or me for allowing it to happen. But I'm on the way there. Not for him. But for myself and Lark."

He led her to the chairs, and she sat, placing her crutches aside. She shook her head to the offered coffee. "I… I'll be going back to the ICU while the lawyers are working on getting me custody of Lark."

He swallowed around the lump in his throat as he wiped her moist cheeks. "You'll be staying by his side?"

"He's dying. Or… it seems like it. But he did manage to talk to the police. He…" She took several breaths, and more tears streamed down her face. "Look at me. I promised I'd never cry for this man again, and here I am. I'm crying for his lost life. For the years of my life spent in vain. For the damage he wanted to inflict on me, and did. For the damage he probably didn't want to inflict on Lark and still did."

Only the footfalls of nurses moving between rooms and the beeping of patients' machines interrupted their moment of silence. Moment of mourning.

Then Jessie, probably the most pragmatic of them, asked, "Did he confess to the police about the kidnapping, deceit, and abuse?"

"To my surprise, yes. Maybe it was to clear his conscience before dying. Or... I don't think he did it for me, but for Lark. He might've never loved me, but he loves his daughter. At least, I hope so." Courtney got up. "I need to go back. I'll hold his hand. Nobody should die alone."

Sean walked alongside her to the room, wishing he could carry her as her crutches struck the hospital tiles, carry her burdens as her shoulders sloped. He'd gladly stay with her by Lowell's bedside. But he suspected it would only worsen the man's condition and might even, well, speed up the process.

So, heart heavy, he returned to his seat.

Jessie waved at the large Christmas tree with twinkling golden lights standing in the corner. "It's three days before Christmas. Let's pray for a miracle."

So they did.

Three hours later, Courtney told them Lowell's condition didn't just stabilize. He started getting better.

Courtney had no clue how to navigate this new stage in her life. Her head was spinning.

How could she explain everything to a four-year-old when she couldn't wrap her own more mature mind around it?

Thanks to Lowell's confession, the DNA results, the family reunification rule, the stellar character references from Courtney's colleagues and clients, *and* the legal team Paisley's network assembled with a shocking speed, Lark had been placed in Courtney's care much faster than Courtney could even hope for. There were still legalities to sort out and a court hearing to go to, but she'd gotten temporary custody.

Lowell had griped that he'd been dying for such a short time but had still managed to do so many stupid things. However, he hadn't asked for custody of Lark and had even let Courtney get Lark's things—with police officers present. Most likely because, in addition to his confession of kidnapping, fraud, and assaulting Courtney, he'd been slammed with accusations of physical abuse and assault from several women once the shooting news appeared on TV and was posted and reshared many times on social media. The women seemed relieved they could tell the truth now and he couldn't hurt them anymore.

Courtney suspected Paisley and her network had a hand in the social media posts going viral and all the reshares, but she'd already learned not to ask. She'd just bought a bunch of things with butterflies on them to give Paisley as Christmas presents.

The much bigger question was how to help heal a traumatized little songbird who'd just been plucked from her nest. Especially considering that Courtney was a stranger to her daughter. She hadn't spent all that much time with Lowell after the death of Naomi, the only mother Lark had known, but another change of parents would surely be a challenge for any child.

Ponies helped. Both the living ones in the stables at the ranch, the plush ones Courtney and Sean had picked up from Lowell's place, then the new one they'd bought her as a Christmas present. Sean's little niece, who'd returned with her parents from their European trip, had become an immediate friend and helped, too. Even Madeline's sweet baby, unknown to the latter, had helped. Lark, smitten, decided they were all sisters.

Yesterday, Courtney had been baking cookies with Sean again, but this time, it was drastically different from before, when she'd nearly soaked the dough with tears. First, because she had a special helper—her daughter. Second, because Courtney wasn't drowning in her sorrow any longer.

And today... today was Christmas.

While Courtney still had hang-ups about her cooking after all Lowell's criticism, she'd helped cook dinner. As she scooped stuffing into a large bowl, her stomach responded to the turkey-and-spice aroma. Her heart responded to the sight of Sean in an apron matching hers as he carved the turkey. He'd bought three sets of several things, with the smallest one being for Lark: aprons, Christmas sweaters, and even socks with pony patterns.

Being a new mom with a four-year-old, Courtney didn't know how to navigate this relationship with Sean. Was there a relationship, even?

Cormac and Declan ventured in and out of the kitchen, picking up ham and mashed potatoes, but they disappeared into the dining room fast as if to give Sean and Courtney privacy.

"I'm gonna help! I'm gonna help!" Lark reached for the gigantic turkey platter on the counter. "I'm gonna carry it to the table!"

Courtney flinched. "No, sweetheart, please."

The girl scrunched her upturned nose. "But, Mommy, you walk on three legs, and your hands are busy. You can't carry things."

Sean moved to the girl. "That's so nice of you to want to help. How about you carry these napkins?"

Courtney sent Sean a grateful glance.

"Okay." Then the little songbird saw Scratcher walking into the kitchen, probably attracted by the turkey smell. "Kitty!" she squealed out her delight.

Courtney flinched again, and while she wasn't concerned about the cat, he seemed to flinch, too.

Napkins and turkey forgotten, Lark lunged at the cat faster than he had the chance to dash—which was pretty fast.

Uh-oh. Terrified that the notorious cat would use his claws on Lark, Courtney rushed to her daughter. "Little birdie, maybe it's better to let the kitty go."

"No, kitty likes me! Look!" Lark hung onto the cat, who had a bewildered expression—probably because he'd realized someone in the household didn't recognize his authority.

To Courtney's utter amazement and probably to the cat's own, Scratcher didn't use a single claw. He didn't look too happy, but he exercised patience Courtney had no clue he possessed.

"It's going to be all right." Sean touched her hand, sending delicious tingles over her skin. "He's not going to hurt her."

Courtney wasn't so sure, but if she tried to take the cat from Lark, the cat might change his mind. Her protective maternal instincts flared up. How did parents do this on a regular basis? How could she protect her little one from harm when Courtney knew firsthand how much harm could be inflicted? How could she become not a helicopter parent but a navigator one, especially when Lark became a teenager?

"You're doing great," Sean said as if reading her thoughts.

Sean's brother's family who lived at the lodge had returned from Germany, and their little girl ran into the kitchen, followed by Paisley. The girls were becoming best buddies fast, and Courtney sent up a prayer of gratitude.

"I got kitty!" Lark showed the cat to her new friend.

"Auntie Paisley! We got the kitty!" Isabella and Lark screamed to Paisley.

Lark seemed to enjoy being showered with attention from so many newly discovered aunts and uncles as she'd adopted the O'Neills as her family, and they didn't protest. Courtney had tried to explain they weren't blood related, but it didn't seem to matter to Lark. Maybe Courtney had been failing as a mother already, and her heart squeezed.

Of all the "aunts," though, Paisley appeared to be both little girls' favorite, maybe because she always smiled and seemed happy to see them. Courtney wouldn't admit it out loud, but Paisley was her new favorite friend, too.

Paisley winked at Courtney, then accompanied the girls to the living room. "You sure did."

"Let's take him to the window. Cats like sunshine," Isabella said with authority.

Not only cats. Courtney exchanged glances with Sean.

"I'm gonna carry him." Lark hugged Scratcher tighter.

Courtney tensed again.

"No, *I* wanna carry him!" Isabella extended her little hands. The butterflies in her hair got askew as if ready to take flight.

Scratcher started looking worried—Courtney knew the feeling—and probably decided that even the entire turkey wasn't worth this.

"The turkey is ready, right?" Grinning, Declan pivoted around the girls, picked up the giant plate, and hurried to the dining room. Maybe he'd already learned that, when females argued, it was best to get out of the way fast.

Sean leaned to the girls. "Why don't you *both* carry the kitty?"

"Okay." There came a bit of a scuffle over who was going to carry which part—both girls seemed to favor the part with the kitty's head and ears—but eventually, they carried Scratcher to the living room window. The cat, apparently not appreciating their selfless efforts, dashed into the hall, then to the open guest room where Courtney had a feeling he might've established a world feline speed and height record in jumping to the closet's top shelf.

"Girls, let's wash your hands. Dinner is ready," Courtney announced before the little ones had the chance to chase the cat.

"Okay."

Courtney took great pleasure in such a mundane task as helping her daughter wash her tiny hands. The liquid soap smelled of jasmine, and when Courtney leaned to kiss the top of her girl's head, Lark's hair smelled of baby shampoo.

Jasmine wasn't Courtney's favorite scent any longer. Now, it was the scent of no-tears baby shampoo.

Courtney led her daughter to a small table set up for the children, reluctant to leave her even for a moment. Never mind that she'd be nearby.

It was as if Lark could be taken away from her again, at any moment.

Sean touched her hand for a fleeting but wonderful moment. "Would you like the girls to sit at the table with us?"

Sean's nephew, also Isabella's teen brother, looked up from the table where he helped his sister settle in and adjusted the butterfly clasps in her hair. "Don't worry, Ms. Rogers. I'll take care of both girls."

"I got the best brother in the world!" Isabella beamed.

"I wanna sit with Isabella and her brother." Lark pouted.

Courtney paused, taking a slow breath. "It's okay, Sean."

"We is gonna have presents soon, right?" Lark grinned.

"Right, darling." Gratitude swelled in her chest again. The O'Neill family really came through and had wrapped up lots of presents for Lark and some for Courtney. But the biggest present was having Lark and Sean this Christmas.

Best present ever.

She winced at the memory but then leaned into the moment and into Sean who pulled out the chair at the adults' table for her.

What was a huge present, as well, was that her songbird had seemed to accept her as her new Mommy and asked for her father less. It wasn't going to be easy, and Courtney wasn't going to try to erase Lark's father from the girl's life or tell her a single bad word about her daddy. But it was progress.

Courtney sat, still not sure she'd done a good job explaining what had happened to Lowell. Because how could one explain that situation?

This was the first Christmas in years—ever?—Courtney would spend with a lot of people. During her marriage, she'd spent plenty of holidays alone.

An incoming text beeped her phone. She shouldn't look, but she checked it fast.

It was from her mother. Neither Courtney's mother nor sister had answered Courtney's calls yet, so she'd texted, wishing them a Merry Christmas. Neither had called back, but there was a text from her mother.

Merry Christmas.

Courtney smiled. More progress.

She stole a glance at Lark, who was busy chatting with Isabella. Worry for her little girl still clenched Courtney's stomach. Lark had cried for her daddy at first and would probably be asking for him again soon.

Courtney and Sean had taken Lark to a child psychologist and lined up more appointments. It wouldn't have been easy to get these appointments so close to the holidays and on such short notice, but Sean's family had seemed to call in favors.

Courtney turned away from the children's table and placed one hand in Sean's and another one in Paisley's.

"She'll be all right," Sean whispered in Courtney's ear, his hot breath sending a delicious tingle over her nerve endings.

"I'll say grace," his father said, making everyone look up and pay attention.

As Courtney listened to the beautiful words, her heart swelled with gratitude for all the unexpected blessings. Being here with Lark and Sean and his family was a true Christmas miracle. Many of them, actually. Having heard the testimonies of the other women Lowell had abused, Courtney knew now that even being alive was a Christmas miracle. Her heart shifted.

After praying in the hospital for the man who'd hurt her so much, she hadn't become a devout Christian overnight. But she'd started the journey. And as her hand lay in Sean's, she knew he'd help her every step of the way.

"Amen," everyone said, and she echoed it, as well.

Then they got busy serving the food and helping each other. She glanced back, grateful to see Isabella's brother filling plates for both girls and cutting their food for them.

Sean lifted the carafe toward Courtney. "Would you like some lemonade?"

"Yes, please." She glanced at her distorted reflection in the carafe before he poured the liquid into her glass. She'd had a distorted vision of herself for such a long time, deliberately changed by Lowell to keep her under his thumb.

Helpless. Dumb. Uneducated. Unsophisticated. Scared. Constantly afraid of saying the wrong thing. Doing the wrong thing. Apologizing for her very existence.

That vision of herself had started changing after her divorce. But seeing her reflection in Sean's eyes, trying to look at herself through the prism of praise and admiration he'd looked at her with, helped the most.

Sean seemed grateful for her very existence, and that was one of the most intoxicating feelings in the world.

With her approval, he piled food on her plate.

"I'll be right back." She checked on her daughter, who seemed to be doing well and eating well. Lark played with her toy planes and a little plastic pony, one of the Christmas gifts Sean had given her.

As Courtney returned, she joined the conversation at the table led by Declan about his international travels. After a brief hesitation, she added her experiences, holding her fork and her head high.

"How awesome to have seen so much," Genevieve said with clear admiration in her voice.

Everyone agreed.

"It takes a lot to be a pilot. We're so proud of you," Sean's mom said, and everyone agreed again.

Courtney straightened her newly polished spine to its full capacity as she munched on turkey and cranberry sauce. Lowell had never seemed to care about what she'd had to contribute to dinner conversation, but people listened to her here.

She'd finally discovered that she mattered. Paisley had been right. It was all about finding the right people. The right people to matter to, and the first people on that list were Lark and Sean.

He grinned at her, and her heart melted faster than butter on her dinner roll.

No, that was wrong. Well, her heart did melt in Sean's presence, but one of the first people on the list of the right people to matter to was herself.

She glanced at Lark again, then tried the yummy ham, mashed potatoes, and bean casserole with cream of mushroom and French onions.

Sean leaned to her, his breath caressing her skin and sending her heartbeat into overdrive. "Everything is delicious. Thank you so much for helping make this dinner."

"It was truly my pleasure. I love..." She nearly said *"I love you"* but pivoted in time. "I love being here. It's more than I could ever dream for."

She took several more bites of the soft roll and then ham, and her taste buds danced in delight.

He touched her hand, causing her heart to skip a beat. "And I love you..." The words nearly made her heart stop as his gaze lingered on her. "I love you and Lark being here. It's more than I could ever dream for, too."

Once again, she forgot about the people around them, and the buzz of conversation disappeared in her ears, replaced by her rapid heartbeat. "What, um, are you trying to say?"

"I–I know that once the cast comes off, you'll return to your job. But if there's a way you wouldn't leave us... I mean, I don't want to tie you down. I want you to achieve all your dreams. But, well, I–I don't want you to go." Then he hurried to add, "Ada would miss you."

The corners of Courtney's lips lifted, but she hid it behind her lemonade glass. "Only Ada?"

"Well, everyone will miss you." Emotion gleamed in his oh-so-rich brown eyes. "Especially... especially me."

She clattered her fork back on her plate. "I'd miss you, too. And I don't want to."

He swallowed hard, based on the movement of his neck. "You–you don't want to miss me?"

Argh. She forked some turkey. Apparently, she and the turkey had the same level of communication skills, but she didn't have the excuse of, well, not being alive. "That came out wrong. I mean, I don't want to have to miss people anymore like I had to miss my mother and sister when I was married to Lowell. Or when I thought I'd lost Lark. I don't want to be far away from people who... who are dear to me." Lark and Sean and what felt like her new family. Maybe she'd be able to fly out of the local airport. As she'd found out recently, the world wasn't such a big place.

His face lit up. "Do you mean that—never mind. I'd love to help as much as I can with Lark while you work. And before that, too. My parents will gladly do the same. They adore her. She's part of the family now. And so are you."

"Thank you. That means a lot. Paisley and Genevieve volunteered to babysit, as well, which I appreciate tremendously." Courtney glanced at her smiling daughter, and her chest expanded again. She took a hurried sip of her cold, tangy drink. Then she realized something. "I was wrong."

His face fell. "Y–you don't like being here? Or you don't want to be close to us?"

She nearly chuckled. She and Sean really needed to work on improving their communication skills, but they'd get there eventually. Maybe because they'd learn to communicate without words. "No, I do. I mean, there's one more thing I could wish for. But I'm afraid to say it out loud yet."

His gaze was understanding, and he let it be. Unlike Lowell who'd prod her until she revealed any secret thoughts or hopes that he'd later use against her.

"Then maybe you should pray for it?" Sean said.

"Yes." She silently prayed for one more Christmas miracle. Maybe it was a selfish prayer. She was new to this, so she didn't know which prayers were selfish yet. She'd learned not to ask much from people, but one could ask for a lot from God, right?

She loved Sean, but she hadn't told him yet because, nearly all her life, her love and devotion had been used against her. With all her heart, she wanted him to love her back. She longed to be a real family with Lark and him.

Was it too much to ask for this Christmas miracle?

Chapter Nineteen

Sean swallowed hard, his nerves getting the best of him as he waited for Courtney to return from a shopping trip with Paisley and Courtney's little daughter.

Genevieve and Madeline had left after helping him decorate and giving him many words of encouragement.

"Hmm, I don't remember ever being this nervous," he whispered into Ada's ear.

Ada barked back, probably nervous, too.

Sean hugged her. "You know you play an important role in this. I wouldn't be able to do this without you. And yes, you'll likely do a better job than I will."

Wearing a giant bow around her neck, the German shepherd licked Sean's hand in response. She clearly agreed with all three statements. Then she squirmed out of the embrace, and he let her go.

He breathed the aroma coming from snowdrops covering the living room floor with white bell-shaped flowers. Nearby, twin rows of jasmine-scented white candles emanated a subtle aroma. A massive white wicker basket held winter jasmine with sunshine-yellow flowers.

That was only part of the scene. Sean, Genevieve, and Madeline, as well as his brothers, spent hours making paper airplanes from colored paper, and he'd written small notes on them. He'd never been great at expressing himself. Had he managed to express himself well enough now?

Would Courtney like this?

His heart skipped a beat. Was it all too simplistic? Should he have hired an airplane to display a banner in the sky? Or a pilot to take them both to the sky she loved so much?

With all his heart, he wanted to make her happy, but he still didn't know how.

She'd told him she loved him, which still made his heart sing, but would she ever be ready for marriage again? Considering how horrible her first one was, how could she be?

And would she deem him a good parent for Lark? The child seemed to accept him easily, but did that mean she'd accept him as a father figure?

Too many questions assaulted him, and he didn't know how to answer any of them.

"What if she says no? Then returns to her home? What if I never see her again?" he asked Ada.

She didn't pay attention but wobbled toward the winter jasmine basket, sniffed it, sneezed, tumbled back, and sat on her behind. Then she looked up at him with a puzzled expression.

He scratched the dog's head. "You don't know it yet, but our lives might be changed forever today."

The low whir of a car motor made them both look up. Ada ran to the hall and nearly slid on the hardwood in her enthusiasm. His heart beating fast, Sean went to greet the love of his life.

Laughter entered his ranch house seconds before Courtney and her daughter did. His heart constricted. Her laughter was music to his ears. When he met her and especially after the brutal assault, he'd dreamed of hearing her laugh.

Together with a breath of fresh, frosty air, she entered the house, holding her four-year-old daughter's hand. Pigtails poked from Lark's pink hat, and curious blue eyes looked up at him. He needed to help them with their parkas, but his feet seemed glued to the oak floor.

He'd thought about all the words he was going to say for days, and yet once again, he was speechless. She stole his breath away.

"Hello, Mr. Sean." Then Lark squealed, "Ooh, you got the dog!"

"Hi, Sean." Cold pinked their cheeks, and Courtney looked like the most beautiful woman in the world.

"Can I pet her? Can I? Can I?" Lark jumped up and down and clapped. When they'd introduced Ada to Lark previously, the girl had been nervous around the large dog, and they hadn't tried to force her.

He sent Courtney a silent glance asking for permission, and she nodded.

The girl giggled happily and lunged to hug the large canine.

The reaction warmed him while Ada sat and preened, a noble lady soaking up all the attention of her fawning subjects.

Tension roiling in his stomach now, he took Courtney's azure-blue parka and helped the girl out of her pink one while Courtney unzipped her boot.

"Well, it's more like *we* got the dog." He cringed. "Maybe. Or..." Why for once couldn't he explain things clearly?

Confusion clouded Courtney's eyes as she stepped out of her only boot. "*We* did?"

"Well, if you go to the living room, I'll explain everything."

Once she clattered on her crutches to the living room, she gasped at the petals, candles, and giant flower basket, as well as the multitude of paper planes hanging from the ceiling. "Those are beautiful."

Well, he wasn't sure at what in particular she gasped, just that she did. That had to be a good sign, right?

He swallowed hard. "They are for you. The florist said winter jasmine originated in China. In Chinese, its name means 'the flower that welcomes the spring.'" He cleared his throat, perspiration forming on his forehead. How had his brothers managed to make it through this process without breaking a sweat?

"The flower that welcomes the spring," Courtney echoed, her gaze pensive.

While Lark hugged Ada, he grasped Courtney's hands and looked into her eyes. "*You're* my spring. You're the promise of love and revival and everything beautiful in nature. But I want you to be my every season. I want to meet every season with you. To spend the most precious moments of my life with you. Now and forever."

Courtney's eyes widened. In surprise? Fear? Anticipation? "What are you saying?"

"I'm not great at saying words. So I, um, did my best to write down my thoughts. Why don't you read what's written on the paper planes?"

Her forehead wrinkled. "Oh. There's something written on them?"

"Yes." His heart thudded.

She started unfolding paper airplanes and reading out loud. "'I love the kindness in your blue eyes and the way they light up when you smile.'" She opened another one, her eyes lighting up indeed. "'I love that you still believe in people after everything that happened to you.'" Then another one. "'I love the fierce way your heart fights for others.'" And another one. "'I love your courage. You're a true inspiration.'"

"I'm not just saying those words because I want to win your heart and keep it, though there's that. I'm saying them because they're true." Then he leaned to the girl. "May I borrow the dog for a moment?"

"Um…" Lark pouted but released Ada.

Sean untied the apple-red bow on Ada's neck, and a red velvet box fell into his hand.

As if after a job well done, Ada ran back to Lark and licked her face, making her squeal in delight again. Ada's tail wagged, and Lark giggled.

He dropped on one knee. "I love you, Courtney. I'll always love you. I know your passion is flying, so I'll follow you wherever you go." He coughed a little. "Okay, maybe not into the sky but in moving to a new location."

Then he remembered an important part and shifted toward Lark who was now playing with Ada on the carpet. "Lark, would you be okay if I married your mother and lived together with you?" He wasn't proud of himself, but he needed all the help he could get—even if it meant going a bit underhanded. "We've got ponies. And soon, we'll have baby horses and cows."

"Baby horses! Baby cows!" Lark squealed. Then the little girl blinked. "Will you be my new daddy?"

He prayed for the right words as tenderness toward the daughter he'd never had filled his heart. "I'll be someone who loves you like a daddy. But you don't have to call me daddy if you don't want to."

Her lower lip trembling, the girl turned to her mother. "If I get a new daddy, will you be leaving?"

Somehow, it stayed in the girl's brain that she could have only one parent at a time, so gaining a new one meant losing the previous one. It stabbed Sean's heart. Maybe it wasn't right on his part to shake Lark's world again.

Courtney's blue eyes welled with tears. "Of course not, sweetie. I'll be with you."

"Can I play with the dog then?" Lark grinned at them. "Pwetty pwetty please?"

He asked Courtney the silent question again.

She wiggled a finger at him. "Bribing a child, I see."

Heat crept up his neck. "Okay, I shouldn't have done that."

Courtney laughed. "You're forgiven."

"Can I play with the dog then?" Lark asked, louder this time.

"Yes." Courtney smiled at her child, affection shining in her eyes.

"I love you, Mommy!" Lark squealed and ran to hug her mother.

"Love you, too, Songbird." A blissful expression spread over Courtney's face as she hugged her little girl.

Tenderness filled Sean. Then the realization hit. Courtney didn't answer his question. Did it mean that... The thought of losing her and Lark nearly brought him to his knees—or rather would have if he wasn't already on one.

Lark ran to play with Ada on the carpet again, her joyful expression priceless.

Courtney touched his shoulder. "You're my spring, too. You reawakened me to life. You *saved* my life. You showed me that renewal is possible. That I matter. You're my every season, as well."

Her words meant the world to him. But she didn't continue.

Uh-oh. His heart dropped. "But...?" he prompted.

She chuckled. "There's no *but*."

"You didn't answer my question." And it was crushing him.

Courtney laughed. "You never asked it."

Even Ada covered her head with a paw in embarrassment.

Heat reached his ears. "Oh. That's right. Will you marry me and make me the happiest man alive?"

"Yes! And we don't need to move anywhere."

His heart soaring, he slipped the ring on her finger, then jumped to his feet. Ecstatic, he lifted her and whirled her around.

Lark leaped to her feet and clapped. "We're gonna be a family!"

Just to be on the safe side, he whispered in Courtney's ear. "You didn't just say yes because of the dog and the ponies I promised Lark, right?"

She laughed again, and her eyes sparkled. "Right. But they did help"—she pinched two fingers together—"just a little."

Epilogue

A month and a half later...

"Look at you! You're glowing."

On Valentine's Day, Courtney laughed as Genevieve rearranged Courtney's veil in the small dressing room off the church. The room smelled of snowdrops and winter jasmine from her bridal and bridesmaid's bouquets. The church was new to her, but Sean had gone here since he'd been a little boy.

"Thank you." Courtney put on white boots and zipped them up, grateful to be able to walk on both legs and wear both boots. She'd never take full mobility for granted again.

She peered at her smiling reflection. For so many years, she'd avoided looking in the mirror because she didn't want to see bruises on her face and fear in her eyes. She'd rarely smiled, except when she'd had to pretend for Lowell as he didn't like gloomy faces.

Her chest swelled. She smiled a lot now. Her skin looked much healthier. And the happy woman in the mirror, standing tall, looked like a new person, nothing like the miserable one she'd once been. Because she *was* a totally new person.

That was what unconditional love could do to a person. How amazing to love and be loved like she'd experienced with Sean. For the first time in her life.

She picked up the maid-of-honor bouquet, breathed the scent of jasmine in deeper, and handed it to her sister, Monica. "Thank you for agreeing to be my maid of honor and helping with the wedding."

Yes, Paisley, who'd become a good friend over the past weeks or one of her foster sisters, soon to be Courtney's sisters-in-law, would've stepped into this role. And it would be impossible to erase many years of hurt between her and her sister in a month. Or ever.

Courtney had pushed her mother and sister away, and neither one of them would forget it. They might never become one happy close-knit family like the O'Neills were. But at least her mother and sister were willing to try to mend the bridge she was building toward them anew.

"It was my honor. Literally. I don't think I've ever seen you this happy," Monica said quietly. "Well, maybe except a couple of times as a little girl during Christmas. No, you look happier now."

Courtney hesitated, then hugged her sister.

Once she stepped back, her mother handed her the bridal bouquet. As it was a winter wedding, Courtney had decided to go with a white and yellow theme, like snow and sun, so the snowdrops and jasmine flowers had the perfect colors. "Monica is right. You look much happier than even before you opened gifts at Christmas as a child."

The best gift ever.

Courtney flinched and clutched the bouquet so tight something stuck in her finger. She loosened her grip and lifted her head. She had to let this go. This was truly the happiest day of her life, and she couldn't allow past misery to ruin it. She was getting married to the man she loved with her whole heart, and that heart shifted in her chest.

What could be better?

As if to answer her question, the door opened, and Lark ran in, followed by Paisley, who was a bridesmaid *and* Lark's nanny for the day. Like Genevieve and Monica, Paisley was wearing a pale-yellow dress and white boots. But the headband with canary-yellow butterflies pushing back her pink-azure hair and her hair itself were some of the many things that made her unique.

Lark shouted, "Mommy, Mommy, do I look pwetty?"

This—this couldn't be better. Love filled Courtney so much it was overwhelming. It was a miracle Lark had accepted her as "Mommy," a true gift Courtney would treasure forever. As well as the fact that Lark hadn't been asking for Daddy any longer and had taken a shine to Sean.

Courtney's new family was truly "the best gift ever."

"You're the prettiest flower girl ever!" Courtney lifted her little girl, then harrumphed from the weight. She hid her face in the many rosy ruffles that decorated Lark's pink dress.

"Mommy, put me down!" Lark squirmed. "I gotta *wowk* to do." Her darling face scrunched into a serious expression. "Those petals a'en't gonna *spwead* themselves." She pointed at her basket. Her chocolate-brown hair was curlier than Courtney's, and those curls bounced together with pink bows woven in.

"You're right. It's a very important job, and thank you for agreeing to do it." Courtney laughed as she placed her daughter on the floor. She could laugh now easily and without her sides hurting. Another huge blessing. "Love you, Songbird."

"Love you, too, Mommy." Lark skedaddled out of the room together with Paisley.

"I still can't believe I have a grandchild," Mom whispered. "She looks just like you when you were little." Then her mother clapped. "It's time."

It was, and Courtney's heart started beating wildly. It was more than she could wish for. Her future in-laws had kindly volunteered their barn for the reception, and Genevieve, Paisley, Monica, and Courtney's mother had helped decorate it with pine branches and white and yellow bells and accents.

"Genevieve, I truly appreciate everything you've all done in helping organize this."

Genevieve rolled her eyes. "Of course! You're family, and we love you. We're happy to help you."

Her mother's eyes flashed, then dimmed. Or maybe Courtney only imagined that. Having endured her own abusive marriage, Courtney understood even better what their mother had gone through.

After hugging Courtney, Monica left the room first, followed by Genevieve. Until it was only Courtney and her mother left.

Tears appeared in her mom's eyes. "I'm so sorry that I let you push me away. That I didn't see through Lowell's deception and manipulation. That I let you and Monica go through your father's abuse as children."

Courtney hugged her mother. "It's in the past. I want to have a relationship with you. And I want Lark to have two wonderful grandmas and a fabulous grandpa."

"Thank you." Once Courtney let her go, her mom wiped her tears. "We'd better go. I don't want Sean to start worrying."

"Oh, he knows I'm not going to be a runaway bride." Courtney chuckled as she placed her hand in the crook of her mother's arm. "But you're right. We'd better go."

Euphoria filled her every cell as she walked down the aisle, reunited with her mother who was giving her away. Her sister and new sisters-in-law decorated the pews with white and pale-yellow bows, and the church was filled with people of the small town who knew and loved her new family and who'd taken her in as one of their own. She'd never experienced a sense of community like she did here. And her darling daughter was grinning at her from the end of the aisle, Paisley's hand keeping the girl in place.

Beaming, Sean was waiting for Courtney, and she had to pace herself while she wanted to fly to him and fling herself into his arms.

Happy tears blurred her vision. She shouldn't compare this wedding to her first one. But as she walked, she couldn't help thinking how different they were. Before her first wedding, she'd had doubts based on the signs she'd picked up but refused to believe. Now, she had an absolute certainty she wanted to marry this man.

To spend a lifetime with him. Now and forever.

THE END

From Alexa: If you'd like to know what happened to the foster sisters and their new families later (and have an option to subscribe to my newsletter), please click **here**[1]. Thank you so much for reading the Escape to Cowboy Crossing series! It means a lot to me.

---

1. **https://bookhip.com/WHDKQLA**

Sugar Cookie Recipe

<u>Ingredients</u>

- 3 eggs
- 1 cup (230 g) shortening or butter
- Vanilla, to taste
- 1 cup (200 g) sugar
- 1 pinch of salt
- 2 tsp (10 g) baking powder
- 2–3 cups (250–375 g) flour

<u>Procedure</u>

1. In a large bowl, beat eggs lightly to break the yolks as one would for scrambled eggs, then mix in the shortening. If using butter, soften it slightly beforehand by heating it a little. The shortening/egg mixture should be loose.
2. Mix in the sugar, then add the salt to the liquid mixture.
3. Add the baking powder, then slowly add the flour as needed to reach a proper doughy state (in essence, able to be shaped without sticking to one's hands too much). You may not need all of the flour, or you may even need a little more based on your eggs and how closely you measured.
4. Make balls and place onto a greased or parchment-lined pan then into an oven heated to 175°C (350°F), and let bake for between 15–20 minutes.

<u>Notes, tips, and variations</u>

- Using three tablespoons of cocoa powder one can get a slight chocolate flavor to the cookie, without being overtly chocolatey.

- Try adding chocolate chips to the dough.

● Approximately 1 teaspoon of vanilla extract works well for this recipe.

● Adding some cinnamon and nutmeg gives a good flavor.

● When heating up the butter, make sure that it's only barely solid when it's mixed into the eggs.

Source: https://en.m.wikibooks.org/wiki/ Cookbook:Soft_Sugar_Cookies (public domain). Not quite the same recipe Sean and Courtney used, which I can't share here for copyright reasons!

Other books by Alexa Verde

To see an updated list of all my other books or subscribe to my weekly reader newsletter (and get a free ebook as your welcome gift!) click here[1].

1. https://www.subscribepage.com/alexaverdepublishedbooks

Acknowledgments

First of all, thank You to God for putting up with me, and for all the blessings!

A million thanks to you, my readers, for reading my books, for sending me encouragement, and for supporting me.

Many thanks to my street team, Alexa's Amazing Readers, and to my beta readers, whom I love to pieces. Special thanks to Kim, Carol, Julie, Margaret, MaryEllen, Terry, Mary Jane, and Trudy for their feedback and help with typo-spotting!

Heartfelt thanks to author Jessie Gussman for coming up with the idea for the Cowboy Crossing series and for helping me so much on the way. Jessie, you make me laugh, you make me smile, and you make the world a better place.

I also thank my wonderful editor, Deirdre, for coming through for me every time.

9 798223 699637